THE WHISTLING CAME FIRST

THE WHISTLING CAME FIRST

COLEMAN HARPER

Blerd Corner

Published by
Blerd Corner, LLC
A subsidiary of OmniSpectrum Media Group, LLC
First Edition: March 2026
Printed in the United States of America

ISBN: 979-8-9954230-0-3 (E-Book-EPUB)
ISBN: 979-8-9954230-1-0 (E-Book-Adobe PDF)
ISBN: 979-8-9954230-4-1 (Paperback)
ISBN: 979-8-9954230-5-8 (Hardback)

Acknowledgments

This story lived in my head for a long time before I ever let it touch the page. Getting it out—and getting it right—wasn't a solo run. A lot of people held me up when life was life-ing, and when I was deep in the work trying to make sure the story felt true.

To my wife, Kimberly: you're the foundation. You believed in this before I could explain it. The Otherlight Universe exists because you never stopped seeing what I was trying to build—even when it was still just smoke, discussion around the house about what you were reading, and the laughs.

To Ann Marie Casey: my creative collaborating partner—thank you for pushing me to finally release this story. It needed to be told, and you wouldn't let me leave it sitting in the dark.

To Josiah J. Jones of J Cube: thank you for bringing a sharp eye and a writer's instincts to this manuscript. You helped tighten it up and make it stronger without stripping the soul out of it.

To Damien Woodard of AWOE: thank you for seeing the vision and trusting it enough to put your hand on it. The cover is the first thing people will see of this universe, and you understood what that meant without me having to explain it twice.

To my family and friends: thank you for the patience, the support, the check-ins, and for listening to me ramble about what I was building creatively—and for not brushing it off like it was "just an idea." I can't name everybody, but I don't take any of it lightly. Your faith carried me.

And to the readers: Mastonia never existed, it's a fictional town. But the things it's built from are real: memory, place, community, and the kind of silence that settles when people decide not to look too closely. I wrote this story because some silences need to be broken. The fact that you're here with it means everything.

Prologue

This story takes place in Mastonia, Arkansas, in 1926
—
a forgotten town resting in the shadow of the Ouachita
Mountains.
Founded in the 1870s, Mastonia was once a prosperous
railroad town,
built by Black families carving out life, dignity, and own-
ership
in a world that offered little of any.
The trains are gone now.
The town is gone.
All that remains is a marker.
The graves have no names.
No dates.
No stones to say who lies beneath.
Time did what violence could not finish.
Nature closed her hands around the land and took it
back—
trees where homes once stood,
roots where memories were buried.
In Otherlight places do not die.
They remember.
And Mastonia still remembers everything.

***

Quartz crystal.
Rare.
Beautiful.
Exploited.
Pulled from the earth like buried stories.

***

They called him the Whistling Man because no one ever learned his real name.

When he finally stepped into view, he was a Black man the color of midnight— not shadow, not absence, but depth.

As if the night itself had learned how to stand upright.

He was beautiful.

Too beautiful.

The kind of beautiful that made you look twice— not out of admiration, but confusion.

His suit never wrinkled.

His shoes never dulled.

Even in the red clay heat of August, he never sweated.

Not once.

His teeth were pearly white.

Too white.

Too even.

They caught the light when he smiled— and he smiled often.

Not wide.

Not cruel.

Just enough to suggest he knew something you didn't.

Something already decided.

His eyes never rushed.

They lingered.

Measuring.

And afterward, no one could agree on their color.

When he spoke, his voice was smooth— warm even— the kind that made people lean in without realizing they had moved.

But if you listened close, there was no breath behind it.

No rise. No fall.

Just sound, arriving.

He laughed easily.

Worked a room without effort.

Carried himself like someone who belonged everywhere.

Dogs went quiet when he passed.

Children stared too long.

Old women crossed themselves and couldn't say why.

The whistle came first.

Always the whistle.

Low.

Unhurried.

A sound that slid beneath doors and into dreams.

He spoke of opportunity like it was generosity.

Spoke of progress like it was inevitable.

Spoke of the mountains as if they had confided in him alone.

And when he grinned—
those perfect teeth flashing against that endless dark— it felt like a confession wrapped in charm.

Some said he was just a man.

Some said he was a devil in good boots and better manners.

Others said he was worse— because the devil, at least, never pretends he isn't enjoying the work.

The Whistling Man never raised his voice.

Never dirtied his hands.

Never stayed long.

He only pointed.

Suggested.

Smiled.

And long after he left— after the land was stripped, after the town went quiet— people swore they could still hear that whistle.

Not as a warning.

But as a reminder.

In Otherlight, evil doesn't always arrive breathing fire.

Sometimes it comes looking like you.

Sounding like promise.

Smiling like it already won.

* * *

Part One: The Town Alive

***

1

The Keeper

T he heat sat on Mastonia like a hand that didn't ask permission. But the town was used to things that didn't ask.

Etta Mae Crawford wiped her forehead with the back of her wrist and turned another page of her ledger, the leather cover worn soft from forty years of handling. Across the table, Mother Jessup was still talking—had been talking for the better part of an hour—her voice rising and falling like creek water over stones.

"—and that's when Cornelius said to the man, he said, 'Sir, I don't know what you paid for that mule, but you were robbed twice: once for the money and once for the trouble.' And the whole market just fell out, Etta Mae. Fell out laughing. You could hear it all the way to the rail station."

Etta Mae smiled, her pen moving steadily. At sixty-two, her hands weren't as steady as they'd once been, but they still knew this work—the careful loops of letters, the weight of a name pressed into paper. She'd been keeping the ledger since she was twenty-two, when her grandmother had placed the blank book in her hands and said, Someone has to remember.

Someone has to write it down.

That first morning, Etta Mae had sat in this same position—different chair, different table, but the same quality of light slanting through a window—and felt the weight of the empty pages like a physical thing pressing against her chest. Her grandmother's hands had guided hers through the first entry. The ink had smelled of iron and oak galls, dark as old blood, and when the nib touched the page it made a sound like a whisper beginning. Her grandmother had mixed that ink herself from a recipe passed down through three generations, a recipe that started somewhere across the ocean in a place that had different names now, a place her grandmother's grandmother had been stolen from before anyone thought to write down exactly where.

The pen she used now was the third one. The first had belonged to her grandmother—a simple wooden holder with a steel nib that had to be dipped every few words. That one rested in a velvet-lined box in Etta Mae's bedroom, too precious for daily use. The second had been a gift from Samuel, Sonny Ray's brother, before he went north. He'd saved for months to buy it—a proper fountain pen from a catalog, the kind white folks used. She'd written with it for fifteen years until the mechanism wore out, and now it sat beside the first in that same velvet box, keeping company with ghosts.

This pen was practical. Steel nib, wooden holder, nothing fancy. But it did the work. The work was what mattered—not the prettiness of the tool but the permanence of what it left behind.

"Cornelius always did have a mouth on him," Mother Jessup said, softer now. "Lord, I miss that man."

"He's in here now." Etta Mae turned the ledger so the old woman could see. "Right next to your wedding date and the year your first child was born.

He's not going anywhere."

Mother Jessup reached out and touched the page with trembling fingers. The ink was still wet.

"You do good work, child," she said. Even at eighty-one, she still called Etta Mae "child." Everyone did. The Keeper of Names was everyone's child, everyone's responsibility. "Holy work."

Through the open window, the sounds of Mastonia drifted in: the clang of Silas at his forge, children's voices from the direction of the schoolhouse, the rhythmic thump of someone beating a rug on a porch rail. A warm breeze carried the smell of pine resin and honeysuckle and the faint mineral tang of the creek.

On the windowsill, a chunk of quartz caught the afternoon light.

Etta Mae's eyes lingered on it longer than usual. Mother Jessup had given her that piece years ago—pulled from the creekbed after a hard rain, when the water ran fast enough to turn up what the earth had buried. It wasn't the clearest crystal, not the kind the rock hunters from Hot Springs paid money for. But it held light in a particular way, throwing small rainbows across the kitchen when the sun hit it just right. Her grandmother had believed the quartz remembered things—that if you sang into a crystal, your voice would live there forever, echoing in the stone's heart long after your throat had gone to dust. Etta Mae wasn't sure she believed that. But she kept the crystal anyway, and sometimes, late at night when sleep wouldn't come, she held it to her ear and listened for the voices of the dead.

Etta Mae closed her ledger and stood, her knees protesting the hours she'd spent on Mother Jessup's hard kitchen chair. "I should let you rest.

Sonny Ray's expecting me at the store before supper."

"That man." Mother Jessup shook her head, but she was smiling. "Still looking after you after all these years."

"He runs the store. I run the ledger. We have an arrangement."

"Mmm-hmm. Forty years, that arrangement's been running. Some arrangements got a different name."

Etta Mae kissed the old woman's forehead and stepped out into the August heat.

* * *

Mastonia had no official founding date. It had simply accumulated, the way silt accumulates at the bend of a river—slowly, persistently, until one day there was enough to stand on.

The oldest building was the church, built in 1871 by men who had been property six years before. They had hauled the lumber themselves, cut from pines they now owned, and raised the walls in a single weekend while their wives sang hymns and their children played in the red clay dust. The bell had come later—a gift from a white church in Little Rock that was replacing theirs with something larger. It had a crack in it that made the tone slightly flat, but no one in Mastonia minded. They said the crack gave it character. They said it sounded like a voice that had been through something and come out the other side.

The general store had been Sonny Ray's father's before it was Sonny Ray's. The schoolhouse had educated three generations of children who went on to become teachers and doctors and lawyers in cities that had never heard of this place. The blacksmith shop still rang with the sound of Silas's hammer, and the smell of hot iron drifted across the town square on windless afternoons, mixing with woodsmoke and honeysuckle and the particular green scent of the creek.

There was a rhythm to Mastonia that outsiders never understood. The way the women gathered at the well on Tuesday mornings, not because they needed water but because they needed each other. The way the men played dominoes on Ezra's porch every Saturday, the click of tiles punctuating arguments about politics and crops and the inexplicable behavior of wives. The way the whole town fell silent at dusk, just for a moment, as if pausing to acknowledge the day's passage.

Two hundred and thirty-seven souls. That was what Etta Mae's ledger said. Two hundred and thirty-seven people with names and histories and the small daily heroisms that never made it into anyone's record except hers.

She knew them all. She had written them all down.

And she could not shake the feeling that something was coming to take them away.

The road through Mastonia was red clay packed hard by decades of feet and wagon wheels and, once, the iron wheels of trains that no longer came. Etta Mae walked it the way she'd walked it all her life, nodding to faces she knew, calling out names she'd written down.

She thought about Tulsa, like she did sometimes when the sun was too bright and the world felt too fragile. Five years ago, Black Wall Street had burned. Thirty-five blocks of prosperity, gone in a night. She'd written down every name she could find in the papers—the dead, the displaced, the disappeared. It wasn't her town, but it was her people, and she couldn't bear the thought of them being forgotten.

And before that, Elaine. 1919. Just seven years back and barely a hundred miles east. They said between one hundred and eight hundred Black folks had been killed in Phillips County—the number changed depending on who was counting and who was being allowed to count. She'd written those names too, the ones she could find, the ones anyone remembered.

Mastonia had survived. Mastonia had always survived. But Etta Mae knew how thin the walls were between surviving and not.

The heat pressed down on her shoulders like a physical weight. Cicadas screamed from the tree line, their chorus rising and falling in waves that seemed to pulse with the afternoon sun. The red clay dust coated her shoes, worked its way into the creases of her skin, settled on the ledger bag until it looked rust-colored instead of brown. This was the texture of her life— the constant fine grit of this place working its way into everything she touched, everything she was. The land marked you whether you wanted it to or not.

She had thought about leaving, once. Back when she was young enough to believe that somewhere else might be better. Chicago. Detroit. Places where the factories were hiring and a Black woman with good penmanship might find work that paid real money. But her grandmother had looked at her with those ancient eyes and said nothing, and somehow that silence had said everything. The silence had held forty years of keeping. The silence had held a thousand names. The silence had known something about roots that Etta Mae was still learning.

"Afternoon, Deacon Willis."

"Miss Etta Mae." He tipped his hat. He had a suitcase at his feet—Deacon Willis was always heading to the next county for something, lumber or nails or hymnals. Half the time he was gone more than he was home. "How's the ledger?"

"Getting fuller every day."

Henry Bessemer sat on his porch the way he did every afternoon, watching the light change on the ridge. Ninety years had taught him patience. Ninety years had taught him a great many things, most of which he would rather not have learned.

He had been born in a cabin in Georgia with no windows and a dirt floor. His mother had sung to him in a language she was not supposed to know, words she had carried across the ocean in the only place they couldn't be taken from her—the space behind her teeth, the hollow of her throat. She had taught him those songs before she was sold away, and he had kept them the way you keep a coal burning through a long night: carefully, secretly, with the knowledge that everything depended on not letting it go out.

He had been twenty-five when the war came. Twenty-nine when it ended. He remembered the morning the news arrived—remembered the way the overseer's face had gone white as milk, remembered the silence that spread across the fields like something holy. He had walked off that plantation with nothing but the clothes on his back and the songs in his chest, and he had kept walking until he found a place that felt like it might let him stay.

Mastonia had let him stay for fifty-five years now.

Though lately, Mastonia had started to slip. Some mornings Henry woke and couldn't remember if his wife had died last winter or thirty years ago. Some afternoons he found himself standing in the middle of a room with no memory of why he'd come there, the present moment untethered from the moments before it. Time had become a river he couldn't trust— sometimes flowing smooth, sometimes doubling back on itself, sometimes vanishing underground only to resurface somewhere unexpected.

He watched Etta Mae Crawford making her way up the road, her ledger bag over her shoulder, and he raised a hand in greeting. She waved back. Good woman. Doing good work. Writing down the names so they couldn't be erased, the way his mother's name had been erased, the way so many names had been erased before anyone thought to record them.

Henry closed his eyes and let the afternoon sun warm his face. The songs remained, even when everything else clouded and slipped. The songs were older than his memory. They didn't need him to remember them—they remembered themselves, living in his throat the way water lives in a well, always there when you reach for it.

He hummed a few bars of something ancient. The ridge listened. The quartz in the mountain held the sound and kept it.

Past the church with its whitewashed steeple. Past the general store where Sonny Ray was hauling sacks of flour through the side door, his broad shoulders straining against his suspenders despite his fifty-seven years. Past the old Crawford place—her grandmother's house, her house now—with its porch swing and its garden and the chunk of quartz on the threshold that her grandmother had placed there forty years ago, for luck, for memory, for reasons the old woman had never quite explained.

Two children ran past, nearly knocking her into the ditch.

"Isaiah Thibodeaux, you slow down before you break something!"

The boy skidded to a halt, gap-toothed grin flashing. "Sorry, Miss Etta Mae!"

Behind him, Josephine Bell walked at a measured pace, her lips moving silently. Counting steps, probably. The girl counted everything.

"How many today, Josephine?"

"Two hundred and forty-seven from my house to the store," Josephine said. "Two hundred and fiftyone if you go around the mud puddle."

"That's important information. I might have to write that down."

Josephine's serious face broke into something almost like a smile.

Etta Mae watched them go—Marcus already running again, Josephine maintaining her steady pace —and felt the weight of the ledger in her bag. Every name in Mastonia was in those pages. Every birth, every death, every marriage and baptism and story worth remembering. She'd started the ledger forty years ago, convinced that writing things down meant they couldn't be taken from you.

Four decades later, she still believed it.

The leather of the bag had molded itself to her shoulder over the years, shaped itself to the particular curve of her body the way a good shoe shapes to a foot. She could feel the ledger's weight shifting with each step—a solid, comforting presence, like carrying a child on her hip. The book held seventeen hundred and forty-three names now. Some were crossed through—the dead, the moved-away, the vanished. Some had asterisks beside them, notes in her careful hand about things that mattered: first schoolteacher to graduate from normal college, built the bridge over Crooked Creek, delivered three babies during the ice storm of '08. The small facts of lives that would otherwise dissolve into time's great amnesia.

The ridge line to the west was going purple with evening. Somewhere in the hills, the quartz veins that ran through this land like frozen lightning were catching the last of the light.

She shifted the ledger to her other shoulder and walked on toward the store.

* * *

2

The Protector

S onny Ray Williams had hands that could palm a melon and a voice that could gentle a spooked horse. He'd been running Crawford's General Store for thirty-five years—first for the Crawford family, now for Etta Mae herself—and in all that time, he'd never once raised that voice in anger.

He didn't need to. When Sonny Ray said something, people listened.

"You're late," he said as Etta Mae came through the side door, but he was already pouring her a glass of sweet tea from the pitcher he kept behind the counter.

"Mother Jessup had stories."

"Mother Jessup always has stories." He handed her the glass. "That's why you love her."

Etta Mae took a long drink, the sweetness cutting through the dust in her throat. The store was quiet this time of day, the last customers gone home to supper, the shadows lengthening across the wooden floor. Sonny Ray had already swept. He always swept before she arrived, though he'd never admit it was for her.

She studied him in the lamplight—the gray coming into his beard, the stoop that had crept into his shoulders over the past few years. They'd known each other since they were young. She'd been forty-one when Samuel went north.

Samuel. Sonny Ray's younger brother. The charmer, the dreamer, the one who'd been sure Chicago would be different. 1905, that was. Twenty-one years ago. He'd sent letters for three months—full of hope, full of plans—and then silence. Then a telegram. Body found. No witnesses. Case closed.

Sonny Ray had wanted to go north himself, to find whoever had done it, to make someone pay. But their mother had begged him to stay.

Someone has to protect what's left, she'd said. And Sonny Ray had stayed.

He'd been protecting things ever since. The store. The town. Etta Mae herself, though she'd never asked him to.

"You remember that night?" she said suddenly.

"The ice storm, back in '08?"

Sonny Ray looked up. His eyes softened at the edges. "We sat on your grandmother's porch. Couldn't go anywhere, everything frozen solid. You told me what you wanted the ledger to be." Etta Mae could still see it: Sonny Ray at thirty-nine, his breath fogging in the cold, his hands wrapped around a cup of her grandmother's chicory. The ice had coated everything —the porch rails, the bare branches, the whole world gone glass. He'd stayed three days because the roads were impassable, and they'd talked about everything. Everything except what they both knew was there between them.

"A shield," she said. "That's what I called it. A shield against forgetting."

"You said if we wrote everything down, nobody could take it from us. Nobody could pretend we didn't exist."

Etta Mae stared into her tea. "I still believe that."

"I know you do." Sonny Ray's voice was gentle.

"That's why you've been doing it forty years."

The memory sat between them—that cold night, the ice cracking in the trees, two young people who thought words on paper could hold back the darkness.

"Silas said he saw a stranger yesterday," Sonny Ray said. "Walking the old quarry road."

Etta Mae looked up. "What kind of stranger?" "Well-dressed. City clothes." He paused. "Said the man was whistling."

"Lots of men whistle."

"Not like this. Silas said it got into his head. Couldn't shake it all night." Sonny Ray's voice was careful. "Said when he went back this morning to look,

there weren't any footprints. No sign anyone had been there at all."

Through the store window, Etta Mae could see the ridge line, dark now against the fading sky.

"Probably just a surveyor," she said.

"Government men, looking for mineral rights."

"Probably."

But Sonny Ray didn't sound convinced.

* * *

3

The Bone Reader

Delphine Rousseau lived at the edge of town, where the last houses gave way to pine forest and the land began its slow climb toward the ridges. Her cottage was small, neat, surrounded by a garden that grew things other gardens wouldn't.

The people of Mastonia came to Delphine when they needed to know things. Not the things you could look up in books or ask at church. The other things.

She read the bones.

The bones had belonged to her grandmother, and her grandmother's grandmother before that— chicken bones, cleaned and blessed, carried across an ocean in a time before Delphine's family had names that white people could pronounce. Her grandmother had been a mambo in Saint-Domingue. Her mother had been born on a ship. Delphine had been born in a cotton field in Mississippi and had walked to Arkansas with nothing but the bones in her pocket.

She was very old. No one knew how old. Her face was unlined but her eyes held depths that made young men look away and old women cross themselves.

"I've been expecting you," she said when Etta Mae appeared on her porch the next morning.

"The stranger," Etta Mae said. "You've seen something."

Delphine stepped aside to let her in. The cottage smelled of herbs and smoke and something older, something that reminded Etta Mae of the way the quartz veins smelled after a hard rain—mineral and electric and faintly wrong.

The bones were already spread on the table, resting on a cloth so old its original color had faded to something between brown and gray.

"I threw them this morning," Delphine said. "Three times. The pattern was the same each time."

"What did they say?"

Delphine was quiet for a long moment.

"Something is coming," she said finally. "Something old. Older than these bones. Older than the mountains." She looked up. "It walks like a man. It speaks like a man. But it is not a man, child. It has never been a man."

"What does it want?"

"What does anything old want? To be fed. To be acknowledged. To add to its collection."

"Collection of what?"

Delphine didn't answer. She gathered the bones slowly, placing them back in their leather pouch.

"Be careful, child. With your ledger. With your names. Something is coming. And it has been coming for a very long time."

Delphine poured two cups of tea without asking. She always knew when Etta Mae needed tea, the same way she always knew when the weather would turn or when a baby would come early. The cups were chipped at the rims—the same cups they'd been drinking from for thirty years, ever since Delphine's mother had passed and left her the cottage and the bones and the "knowing".

"You remember when your grandmother died?" Delphine said.

Etta Mae's hand tightened on the cup. "You know I do."

"You came to me that night. Walked three miles in the dark, no lamp, no moon. Stood on my porch and didn't say a word. Just stood there shaking."

"I didn't know where else to go."

"I know." Delphine's voice was soft. "I threw the bones for you that night. You remember what they said?"

Etta Mae remembered. She'd been twenty-two years old, orphaned twice over—her parents taken by fever when she was small, her grandmother taken by time just that morning. The ledger had passed to her hands, still warm from her grandmother's touch, and she'd felt the weight of it like a stone pressing on her chest. She hadn't known if she could carry it. Hadn't known if she was strong enough, or wise enough, or steady enough to hold all those names.

"They said I would keep the town," Etta Mae said quietly. "That the names would live as long as I did."

"They said more than that." Delphine reached across the table and took Etta Mae's hand. Her fingers were thin and dry, the bones visible beneath papery skin. "They said you wouldn't do it alone."

Etta Mae looked at the woman who had been her compass for forty years. Delphine had never married, never had children, never wanted either. She had her bones and her "knowing" and her small cottage at the edge of town, and she had Etta Mae, who came to her when the weight got too heavy and the names pressed too hard against the inside of her skull.

"What would I do without you?" Etta Mae asked. She meant it as a joke. It didn't come out that way.

Delphine didn't answer. She just squeezed Etta Mae's hand and looked toward the window, where the afternoon light was starting to fail.

The bones on the table seemed to shift, though neither woman had touched them.

* * *

4

The Church Supper

Sunday came, and with it the smell of fried chicken drifting across Mastonia like a benediction.

The church supper was the oldest tradition in town, older than any living memory. Every family brought something. Every family ate together. At the church supper, everyone was simply from Mastonia. And that was enough.

Etta Mae had brought her grandmother's bread pudding. Sonny Ray had brought a ham from his smokehouse. Delphine had brought nothing, as always, but no one minded.

Across the yard, voices were already rising over the potato salad—the particular pitch that meant someone had brought up something everybody had an opinion about and nobody had a solution for. Deacon Willis and old Thomas Crawford had found their way to the church roof again.

"We've been talking about fixing those shingles for three years," Thomas said. "Three years of leaks. Three years of buckets in the aisle when it rains."

"And three years of not having the money," Deacon Willis replied. "Unless you're offering to pay for it yourself."

"I'm offering to organize a work party. Get the young men together, do it ourselves."

"The young men are leaving. Haven't you noticed? Every season, fewer of them stay."

It was an old argument. Etta Mae let it wash over her—the familiar rhythms of a community debating itself.

The tables were set up in the church yard, under the shade of the oak trees. Children ran between the adults' legs, shrieking with joy. Isaiah Thibodeaux was trying to convince Josephine Bell to climb a tree, and Josephine was explaining exactly how many bones a person could break falling from that particular height.

"Seventeen," she said. "If you fall from that branch. Nineteen if you fall from the higher one."

"How do you know?"

"I counted."

Etta Mae stood at the edge of it all, watching, her heart full of something she couldn't name.

This was Mastonia. Two hundred and thirty-seven souls who had carved a place for themselves in a world that did not want them to exist.

"You're thinking loud thoughts."

Sonny Ray appeared beside her, a plate of food in each hand. He offered her one.

"I'm thinking about what would happen if this all went away," she said.

"It won't."

"Tulsa thought that too. Elaine thought that."

Sonny Ray was quiet for a moment.

"We've survived everything else," he said finally. "We survived the war. We survived

Reconstruction. We survived the Klan coming through in '14 and burning two farms. We survived the influenza." He looked at her. "We'll survive whatever comes next."

"Delphine says something's coming."

"Delphine says a lot of things."

"She's never been wrong. Not completely."

Sonny Ray set down his plate. He took her hand, his palm rough and warm.

"Etta Mae. Whatever's coming—we'll face it the way we face everything. Together. As a community."

* * *

The children were playing a clapping game near the church steps when the silence fell.

It happened all at once—the laughter cutting off, the conversations dying mid-sentence, the clapping hands going still. Even the breeze seemed to stop.

And then: the whistle.

Low. Unhurried. A melody that seemed to come from everywhere and nowhere.

Isaiah Thibodeaux stopped mid-clap. His gap-toothed smile faded. He turned toward the road.

Josephine Bell had stopped counting. Her lips were parted, her eyes wide.

The dogs were not barking. Every dog in Mastonia had gone silent.

And then they saw him.

He came walking up the road from the direction of the quarry, his stride easy, his posture perfect. His suit was black, immaculate, without a

speck of red clay dust. His shoes gleamed. And his skin—

His skin was black in a way that Etta Mae had never seen before. Not brown, not dark, but black like midnight, black like the deepest shadows under the pines.

He was beautiful.

Too beautiful.

He stopped at the edge of the church yard. The whistle stopped with him.

Then he smiled.

His teeth caught the light—white, perfect, too even. His eyes swept over the crowd, lingering on each face. When his gaze passed over Etta Mae, she felt it like a cold wind. When it touched her ledger bag, it seemed to pause.

He did not speak.

He only stood there, smiling, while the silence stretched.

Then he tipped an imaginary hat, turned, and walked back down the road toward town. The whistle started again as he went—low, unhurried, fading into the distance.

No one moved until they couldn't hear it anymore.

Then Isaiah Thibodeaux began to cry.

No one could say why.

* * *

Part Two: The Arrival

***

5

The Offer

Morning came reluctant and gray. Clouds had rolled in overnight, pressing down on the town like a lid on a jar—the kind of low sky that swallowed sound and made distances hard to judge. The air hung thick and wet, carrying the promise of rain that wouldn't fall, just threaten. Somewhere up on the ridge, thunder mumbled to itself like an old man arguing with his memories.

The Whistling Man was already at the general store when Sonny Ray came down to open up.

Sonny Ray had woken before dawn, as he always did, his body trained by decades of early mornings. He'd lain in the narrow bed above the store listening to the building settle around him—the creak of old boards, the tick of wood expanding in the heat, the particular silence of a town holding its breath. Something had kept him in that bed longer than usual. A weight in his chest. A reluctance his mind couldn't name but his body understood perfectly.

When he finally descended the stairs, his hand trailing along the banister worn smooth by forty years of palms, the wrongness announced itself before he reached the door.

The man sat on the porch bench like he owned it. Like he had always been there. Like the bench had been built specifically to hold him, and everything before this moment had been rehearsal.

Sonny Ray's hand froze on the door handle.

Through the glass, he could see the stranger's profile—that impossible stillness, that suit without a single crease despite the humidity that had already plastered Sonny Ray's undershirt to his back. The man wasn't reading. Wasn't whittling. Wasn't doing any of the small fidgeting things that people did when they waited. He simply existed there, as motionless as furniture, as patient as stone.

The door's hinges needed oiling. They screamed into the morning quiet.

The wrongness announced itself in ways his body understood before his mind could name them. The small hairs on his forearms stood upright. His jaw tightened until the muscles ached. Somewhere deep in his belly, in the place where his grandmother had said the spirit lived, something coiled tight as a spring and refused to release. He had felt this way only once before—the night the telegram came about Samuel. That night, he had known something terrible was true before he tore open the yellow envelope. The same knowing pressed against him now, cold and certain.

The morning air should have smelled like dust and coffee and the particular mustiness of the store's wooden shelves.

Instead, it smelled like nothing at all. Like absence. Like a place where smell should be but wasn't. His tongue felt thick and dry, coated with something he couldn't name—not quite copper, not quite stone, but something in between that made him want to spit but couldn't.

His hands had curled into fists without his permission. The nails bit into his palms, leaving crescent moons of pain that were almost welcome— real, physical, ordinary sensations in a moment that felt like nothing ordinary at all.

"Beautiful morning," the stranger said. His head turned—not startled, not acknowledging, just redirecting his attention like a lamp swiveling toward a new subject.

"Is it?" The words came out rougher than Sonny Ray intended. His throat had gone dry. The porch boards groaned under his weight, solid and familiar, and he clung to that sensation—the reality of wood beneath his feet, the smell of dust and old paint, the ordinary architecture of his ordinary life.

"Perspective, friend. It is all about perspective." The stranger stood in one fluid motion, brushing invisible dust from his immaculate suit. His hands were long-fingered and elegant. They moved with the precision of things that had been practiced until they were perfect. "I believe we got off on the wrong foot yesterday. Allow me to introduce myself properly. My name is—"

He said something. His mouth moved. Sound came out.

Sonny Ray felt the name enter his ears, felt it travel toward the part of his brain where names were stored, felt it dissolve like sugar in hot water. There and gone. The shape of it remained for half a heartbeat—three syllables, maybe four—and then nothing. Just the ghost of having heard something he could no longer recall. It was the strangest sensation— not like forgetting, which happened slowly and left edges you could trace. This was more like reaching for something on a shelf and finding the shelf had never existed. His mind kept trying to replay the sound, kept grasping at empty air where a word should have been.

"I represent certain interests," the stranger continued smoothly, as if the impossible thing that had just happened was the most natural transaction in the world. "Interests that see great potential in this region. The quartz deposits in particular. Remarkable quality. Unique resonance. My employers are prepared to offer substantial compensation for mineral rights. Generous compensation. The kind that could transform a small town like this into something... more."

"The land is not for sale."

"Yes, so I have been told. Multiple times. By multiple people. All very protective of their little patch of dirt." The stranger's smile did not waver. It sat on his face like something painted there, technically correct but fundamentally wrong—the smile of someone who had studied smiling without ever understanding what prompted one. "But here is the thing about protection. It only works if you understand what you are protecting against. And I do not think you do. I do not think any of you do."

He leaned closer. His breath should have been warm. It was not. It carried no scent at all—no coffee, no tobacco, no morning staleness, none of the small biological truths that proved a person had woken up and lived through the hours before this moment. Just air, moving from somewhere it should not come from.

Sonny Ray's skin prickled. Every hair on his arms stood at attention. Deep in his gut, in the place where instinct lived older than language, something was screaming at him to run. To get inside. To put walls and doors and distance between himself and this thing wearing a man's shape.

"There are things in those mountains, Mr. Williams. Things that have been there longer than your town. Longer than your people. Longer than anything your history books remember. I am offering you a chance to profit from them before someone else profits from you."

Sonny Ray felt his hands curl into fists. "Get off my porch."

"Of course. I have other people to speak with anyway. Miss Crawford, for instance. The one who keeps the records. I understand she has quite a collection of names." The stranger's eyes glittered. Something moved behind them—not light exactly, but the suggestion of depth, of distance, of spaces that went down and down and never reached bottom. "Names are valuable, Mr. Williams. More valuable than gold. More valuable than crystal. Names are how the universe keeps track of what belongs to whom."

The cold started at the base of his spine and climbed vertebra by vertebra until it reached the base of his skull. His vision narrowed. The edges of the world went gray and strange, like looking through water. He could hear his own heartbeat—too loud, too fast, a rhythm that seemed wrong somehow, syncopated against some other pulse he couldn't identify.

The store around him felt suddenly fragile. The walls that had sheltered goods and gossip for thirty-five years seemed thin as paper, ready to tear at the slightest pressure. The floorboards that had held the weight of a thousand transactions felt soft, uncertain, as if something beneath was hollowing them out from underneath.

He wanted to speak. To shout. To do something that would break the terrible stillness that had settled over everything. But his voice had retreated somewhere deep inside his chest, and when he opened his mouth, nothing came out but breath—if it was breath at all.

He tipped his hat and walked away, that tuneless whistle starting up again, sliding into the morning like oil into water. His footsteps made no sound on the porch boards. No creak. No groan. As if he weighed nothing at all, or weighed so much that the wood had simply given up protesting.

The Whistling Man paused on the road when he saw the old man on the porch.

Henry Bessemer. Ninety years old. Born in bondage, walked into freedom, outlived everyone who had tried to own him. The stranger had collected many

souls in his long existence, but he had never encountered one quite like this.

He watched Henry's eyes—the way they drifted, focused on something that wasn't there, then snapped back to the present. The old man was experiencing time differently. Not the linear progression that made most humans so easy to define, so simple to complete. Henry Bessemer existed in multiple moments simultaneously, his past and present bleeding together, his memories fragmenting and recombining like light through a prism.

It made him difficult to pin down. Difficult to define.

The Whistling Man found this fascinating.

He tipped his hat as he passed. "Good afternoon, Mr. Bessemer."

Henry squinted at him. "Do I know you?"

"Not yet," the stranger said. And then, almost to himself: "I wonder if you ever will."

He walked on, that tuneless whistle starting up again. But he glanced back once. The old man was humming something—something that slipped through the stranger's awareness like water through fingers. Something he couldn't quite hold.

Sonny Ray stood frozen on his porch for a long time. His heart hammering against his ribs. His mind racing through implications he could not quite grasp. The sweat on his back had gone cold. His hands ached from clenching.

He needed to find Etta Mae.

Now.

*　*　*

But Etta Mae was already dealing with her own visitation.

She had woken early to work on the ledger, as she did most mornings. The ritual of it: the creak of the floorboards under her feet, the rasp of the match against the striker, the small bloom of flame touching the lamp wick. The smell of kerosene and old paper and the particular mustiness of a house that had held the same woman for forty years.

The light through her kitchen window was thin and gray, barely enough to write by, but her hands knew the work and her eyes knew the pages. The leather cover fell open to the place she'd marked with a ribbon—red silk, fraying now, a gift from her grandmother on the day she'd inherited the responsibility.

She was recording a birth from the week before. The Miller's third daughter. Opal, they had named her, after the stones that sometimes surfaced in the creek. A good name. A solid name. A name that would hold.

Her pen moved in the careful script she'd perfected over decades. The ink was good—she made it herself from oak galls and iron, the old way, the way that didn't fade. The paper accepted each letter like a promise being made.

Opal Louise Miller, she wrote. Born August 9th, 1926, to James and Dorothea Miller. Third

daughter. Seven pounds, four ounces. Healthy. Named for—

The knock at her door was soft. Almost polite.

Her pen stopped mid-stroke. A drop of ink gathered at the nib, hung there trembling, fell to the page and spread into a small black star.

No one knocked like that in Mastonia. Folks called out as they approached. Rapped hard and familiar. Announced themselves before they even reached the porch. This knock was different. Considered. The knock of someone who understood that doors were barriers and was asking—very formally, very precisely—for the barrier to be removed.

Etta Mae set down her pen. Wiped her hands on her apron. Felt her heart begin to beat in a rhythm she didn't recognize—not fast exactly, but strange, syncopated, as if it were trying to match a frequency coming from outside.

Her grandmother's voice rose up from the deep well of memory: A threshold is a promise, child. What you invite in becomes part of your house. What you keep out stays part of the world. Know the difference.

She crossed to the door. Her hand hovered over the latch. Through the wood, she could feel something—a pressure, a presence, a weight of attention focused on this single point of entry.

She opened it to find the stranger standing on her porch.

His smile was already in place. His eyes already measuring. He stood precisely at the edge of the threshold, his toes aligned with the weathered board that marked the boundary between outside and in, and she understood immediately that this was not accident. He knew. Somehow, impossibly, he knew what her grandmother had taught her about doors and invitations and the architecture of protection.

"Miss Crawford. What an honor. I have heard so much about your work."

Etta Mae did not step back. Did not invite him in. Her body filled the doorframe, shoulder to shoulder, hip to hip.

Behind her, the kitchen waited— the ledger open on the table, the lamp still burning, the ink still wet on Opal Miller's name.

"I do not believe we have met."

"We have not. But I know you all the same.

The Keeper of Names. The Memory of Mastonia. The woman who writes down what others forget." His voice was silk and smoke, winding around her like something trying to find a way inside. "That is important work, Miss Crawford. Sacred work. I have great respect for it."

"State your business."

"Direct. I appreciate that." He did not try to enter. Did not lean forward. Did not do any of the small aggressive things that men sometimes did when they wanted to intimidate. He simply stood there, perfectly still, perfectly patient, as if he had already calculated every possible outcome of this conversation and found them all acceptable. "I am here to make you an offer. A simple trade. Your ledger, in exchange for... well. What would you like? Wealth? Health? Youth?" His smile widened a fraction. "Forgiveness?"

The last word hit her like a slap.

The stranger's words were a cold key turning in a lock Etta Mae had kept oiled and hidden for decades. She didn't see the dusty road of Mastonia anymore; she saw the porch in the Delta, the air thick with the scent of overripe peaches and impending rain. She thought of her sister—the one the ledger could never bring back. She thought of Beatrice's face the last time they'd spoken, the way the light had caught the defiant gap in her front teeth before she turned toward the station and never looked back. To the rest of the world, she was a ghost, but to Etta Mae, Beatrice was the only part of her heart that still refused to be written down.

How could he know? How could anyone know?

"How do you—"

"I know many things, Miss Crawford. Things that are written down. Things that are not. Things that live in the spaces between heartbeats." He reached into his jacket and produced a small piece of quartz. Held it up to the gray light. The crystal caught what little sun filtered through the clouds and threw it back in fractured rainbows that danced across the porch boards, across his face, across the threshold between them. "These mountains remember everything. Every prayer. Every promise. Every name whispered into the dark. All it takes is the right ear to listen."

Etta Mae's hands tightened on the doorframe. The wood was solid under her fingers. Real. Old. It had held this house together for fifty years. It had kept out rain and wind and the small violences of the world. She pressed her palms against it and drew strength from its steadiness.

"The ledger is not mine to give. It belongs to everyone."

"Does it? Or does it belong to no one, which is why you have to protect it? Things that belong to everyone often belong to nothing. Shared property is the easiest to take. All you need is one person willing to sign." He pocketed the quartz. The rainbows vanished. The porch went gray again. "One person willing to say: this is mine to give. This is mine to trade. This burden I have carried all these years—I am ready to set it down."

His eyes found hers. Held them. In their depths, she saw something move—not reflection, not light, but something older. Something that had been watching people from doorways since before doorways existed.

"I am not that person."

"Not yet." He stepped back from the threshold. One step. Two. Giving her space. Giving her the illusion of choice. "But the offer stands, Miss Crawford. It always stands. That is the thing about my kind of business. I am very, very patient."

He turned and walked away. No whistle this time. Just silence, spreading behind him like a stain. His footsteps should have crunched on the gravel path. They did not. His shadow should have stretched behind him in the morning light. It did not. He moved through the world without disturbing it, like a stone sinking through water, like a memory fading from the mind.

Etta Mae closed the door. Locked it. Leaned against it with her heart pounding and her grandmother's voice echoing in her memory:

Someone has to remember. Someone has to write it down.

Otherwise they take it from you and pretend you never existed.

She crossed back to the kitchen table. Sat down heavily in her chair. Looked at the ledger, still open, still waiting. The small black star of spilled ink had dried on the page, marring the entry for Opal Miller.

She picked up her pen. Her hand trembled, but she steadied it. Found her place. Continued writing.

Named for the stones that surface in the creek after heavy rain. May she be as beautiful. May she be as enduring. May she be found when the world needs finding.

She wrote until her hand stopped shaking. Wrote until the gray morning brightened into something almost like day. Wrote until she could no longer hear the silence the stranger had left behind.

* * *

6

The First Night

That night, Mastonia did not sleep.

Etta Mae sat at her grandmother's table with the lamp burning low, the ledger open in front of her. She had not written anything. She did not know what to write.

The quartz on her windowsill glowed faintly in the lamplight.

A knock at the door made her jump.

It was Sonny Ray. His face was drawn, his eyes shadowed.

"You felt it too," he said.

"The whole town felt it."

He came in without being asked, settling into the chair across from her.

"I went to the quarry road after supper," he said finally. "Where Silas said he saw the stranger yesterday."

"Did you find anything?"

"Footprints. Fresh ones, in the dust. Leading into town." He paused. "But none leading out. Like he walked here from nowhere."

Etta Mae thought about that. About a man who appeared without origin, without past.

"Delphine said he's been coming for a long time," she said.

"What does that mean?"

"I don't know." She looked down at the ledger.

"But I think we're going to find out."

* * *

7

The Breaking

The stranger waited a week before he started breaking them.

Not with force. That was not his way. Force was crude. Force created martyrs. Force left evidence that could be pointed to, rallied against, remembered as injustice.

No. He broke them with time. With patience. With the steady, relentless pressure of want.

The days moved strange in Mastonia now. Mornings felt longer than they should. Afternoons compressed into moments. People found themselves standing in the middle of tasks they couldn't remember starting, their hands full of objects they couldn't recall picking up. The town's rhythm had shifted, syncopated, thrown off-beat by the presence that walked its streets without ever seeming to hurry.

Marcus Webb's father died on a Tuesday.

Thomas Webb had been sick for seven months —a consumption that started in his lungs and spread like rot through old wood, hollowing him out breath by breath. The doctors in Little Rock had shaken their heads. Nothing to be done. Just time now. Just waiting.

Marcus had done the waiting. Had sat by his father's bed through the long nights when Thomas's breathing turned to rattling, to gasping, to the terrible silence between attempts. Had held his hand when the skin went papery and thin. Had watched the man who had taught him to plow and plant and stand upright in a world that wanted him bent—watched that man diminish, day by day, until there was nothing left but bones and breath and the fading light behind his eyes.

Thomas died at dawn. Quietly, in his sleep, the way everyone pretended they wanted to go. Marcus was there when it happened. Felt the exact moment when the hand in his went from holding to held. Felt the absence arrive like a door closing in a distant room.

They buried him in the cemetery on the hill, in the plot next to Marcus's mother, who had died bringing him into the world. Reverend Clemmons spoke words that Marcus couldn't hear over the roaring in his ears. Dirt fell on wood. People murmured condolences. The sun was too bright. The sky was too blue. The world had no right to be this beautiful on a day when his father was going into the ground.

The stranger was there at the funeral. Standing at the edge of the crowd. Not speaking. Just watching.

Just... being present.

Everything about him was appropriate—the black suit, the hands folded in front of him, the expression of solemn sympathy on his face. Technically perfect. Fundamentally hollow.

Marcus felt those eyes on him through the entire service. Felt them like a weight. Like a hand resting on his shoulder. Like a voice whispering in his ear: I could have prevented this. I offered. You refused. This is what refusal costs.

That night, Marcus sat alone in the house that felt too big without his father in it. The chair by the fireplace was empty. The pipe on the mantel would never be lit again. The silence pressed against his ears until he thought his head would split from the pressure.

He thought about the offer he had refused. Thought about the snap of fingers. Thought about his name, and whether it was worth what it had cost.

Marcus Webb, he said to himself. Son of Thomas. Grandson of William. Great-great-grandson of—

The names stretched back and back, a chain of men who had lived and died and passed something along. But what good was a chain if the links were made of grief? What good was a legacy if it meant watching everyone you loved slip away while you stood helpless, your hands full of nothing but history?

He was at the boarding house before he realized he had decided to go. The door opened before he knocked, as if the man inside had been expecting him.

The Whistling Man smiled.

"Mr. Webb. I am so sorry for your loss."

Marcus's throat was dry. His hands were shaking. Somewhere in the back of his mind, a voice that sounded like

Etta Mae Crawford was screaming at him to run, to turn around, to go home and grieve like a man instead of crawling to this thing in the dark.

He ignored it.

"The offer," he said. "The one you made at the church. Is it still... is it still available?"

"Offers like mine do not expire, Mr. Webb. They simply wait." The stranger stepped aside. The room behind him was dark, lit only by a single candle that cast shadows in directions shadows should not go.

"Please. Come in. Let us discuss the terms." Marcus Webb crossed the threshold.

The door closed behind him. Hours passed—or what felt like hours. When he came back out, it was almost dawn. He walked home slowly, his step uncertain, like a man navigating a familiar room in the dark. The grief was quieter now. The weight on his chest had eased. He could breathe without the pain catching.

But something else was gone too.

He sat in the chair by the fireplace and tried to remember his father's voice. The words Thomas had spoken—the lessons, the jokes, the quiet encouragements muttered over a plow handle—Marcus knew they had happened. But the sound was gone. The specific timbre, the way Thomas drew out certain vowels, the rumble of his laugh—all of it erased, like chalk wiped from a board. He had the shape of his father. But not the sound.

He told himself it was grief. Told himself memory did this sometimes—took the things you needed most and locked them behind a door you couldn't find. He almost believed it.

For three days, Marcus walked through Mastonia like a man with a hole in his chest that no one could see. He did his work. He nodded to neighbors. But when Etta Mae asked after his father—gently, the way she asked everyone, her pen ready—Marcus opened his mouth and found nothing there. Not silence. Absence. The place where his father's voice should have been, scraped clean.

On the third night, he went back.

This time, the door opened before he knocked. The Whistling Man did not smile. He simply stepped aside, as if he had been counting the hours until this moment. Marcus Webb crossed the threshold a second time.

He did not come back out.

* * *

In the morning, his house stood empty. His fields lay fallow. The chair by his fireplace held no one. The pipe on his mantel gathered dust.

And when people tried to remember his face —really remember it, the specific configuration of features that had made him Marcus and not anyone else—they found the details slipping away. The color of his eyes went first. Then the shape of his jaw. Then the sound of his voice, the way he laughed, the particular rhythm of his walk.

Within three days, even his name had begun to blur at the edges. Folks knew there had been a young man who lived in that house. Knew he had buried his father recently. But when they reached for more— when they tried to call up the weight of his history, the chain of names that connected him to generations past—they found only absence. Only the sense of something that should have been there and wasn't.

"He's started," Etta Mae said when she heard. She was at the general store with Sonny Ray, her ledger open on the counter. Her pen moving fast, racing against forgetting.

Marcus Webb, she wrote. Son of Thomas

Webb. Grandson of William Webb. Last seen August 15, 1926. Went to the stranger twice. The first time he came back without his father's voice. The second time he did not come back at all.

"One man. One name." Sonny Ray's voice was heavy. He stood behind the counter with his hands flat on the wood, as if he needed the support to stay upright. "Maybe that is all he wanted. Maybe he will leave now."

But the stranger did not leave.

One by one, they fell. The desperate. The grieving. The ones whose cracks ran deepest.

* * *

Miss Lillian went next.

The schoolteacher. Thirty-four years old. Unmarried by choice in a world that saw unmarried women as unfinished. She had come to Mastonia from Memphis twelve years ago, fleeing a life that had tried to make her smaller than she was, and had found in this little town a purpose that fit her exactly.

She loved her students. Every single one of them. Loved their questions, their curiosity, their fierce determination to learn despite a world that told them their learning didn't matter. She had watched them grow from children into young people full of promise, full of potential, full of futures that stretched out before them like roads leading to places she could only imagine.

And she had watched them leave.

One by one. Year after year. The bright ones. The talented ones. The ones who could have been doctors and lawyers and professors if the world had been different, if the doors had been open, if the roads had led somewhere other than disappointment.

Some went to cities that chewed them up and spit them out. Some went to colleges that took their money and gave them nothing but debt and disillusionment. Some simply vanished—swallowed by a country that had no place for Black excellence, no room for Black ambition, no patience for Black dreams.

Lillian kept teaching. Kept believing. Kept lighting candles against a darkness that seemed to grow deeper every year.

But the candles were getting harder to light. The belief was getting harder to maintain. And in the quiet hours of the night, when she sat alone in her small house grading papers that would never change anything, she sometimes wondered what the point was.

What the point of any of it was.

The stranger came to her classroom on a Friday afternoon, after the students had gone.

He stood in the doorway, silhouetted against the afternoon sun, and watched her erase the day's lesson from the chalkboard. The scrape of the eraser against slate was the only sound in the room.

"Miss Lillian." His voice was soft. Almost kind. "You work so hard for them."

She did not turn around. "That is what teachers do."

"Yes. But most teachers see results. Most teachers watch their students succeed, build lives, prove that the effort was worth something." He stepped into the classroom. His footsteps made no sound on the wooden floor. "What do you see, Miss Lillian? What has all your work produced?"

She kept erasing. Letter by letter. Word by word. Wiping the board clean so she could fill it again tomorrow with lessons that would make no difference.

"I see children learning," she said. Her voice was steady. Her hand was not. "I see minds opening. I see potential."

"Potential that goes nowhere. Doors that never open. Roads that lead to dead ends." He was beside her now, close enough that she could feel the cold radiating from him like winter through a cracked window. "I could change that, Miss Lillian. I could make sure every student who passes through this classroom finds success. Every test passed. Every opportunity taken. Every door thrown wide open."

The chalk dust hung in the air between them. White particles suspended in shafts of sunlight. For a moment, just a moment, they looked like stars.

"What would it cost?"

"Only what you have already given up on." His smile was gentle. Understanding. The smile of someone who saw her exhaustion and wanted to help. "Only the belief that any of this matters. You have been losing that faith for years, Miss Lillian. I am simply offering to take the last of it. To free you from the burden of hoping for things that will never come."

She turned to look at him then. His face was beautiful. His eyes were deep. And somewhere in those depths, she saw her students—not as they were, but as they could be. Doctors in white coats. Lawyers in courtrooms. Professors at podiums. Living the lives she had dreamed for them, achieving the things she had promised them were possible.

All she had to do was stop believing it could happen on its own.

All she had to do was let him make it true.

She signed something. She must have. There was a moment, a pen, a piece of paper that appeared from nowhere and disappeared the same way.

In the morning, she was still there. Still teaching. Still going through the motions of a life that had been her purpose.

But her eyes had gone flat. Her voice had gone mechanical. She taught lessons from memory, but the passion was gone. The hope. The belief that any of it mattered.

Her students noticed. Of course they did. Children always notice when the light goes out of the adults who are supposed to guide them.

They just didn't know what to do about it.

What none of them knew—what Lillian herself no longer knew—was what she had lost in the exchange. It wasn't just her faith in teaching. It was something older, something deeper. The song she used to sing when the youngest students got scared. The lullaby her mother had sung to her in the fever summers, the one she'd sung back to her mother at the end, holding that thin hand as the breathing slowed and stopped. She had carried that song for thirty years. It had been the thread connecting her to every child she taught, the proof that tenderness could survive even this world.

Now when she tried to remember the melody, there was only silence. When she reached for her mother's face, there was only fog. The stranger had taken the thing that made her teaching mean something—not the skill, not the knowledge, but the love. The love was gone. And Miss Lillian didn't even know it was missing.

* * *

Old Man Thornton was next.

He had been one of the men who raised the church walls in 1871. Not the oldest of them—he had been young then, barely twenty, fresh from a plantation in Alabama with hands that knew nothing but cotton. But the older men had put a hammer in those hands and shown him what they could become. He had learned fast. Learned the way a beam needed to be notched. Learned the angle of a rafter, the bite of a saw through green pine, the particular satisfaction of driving a nail flush with a single stroke. His hands had built half of Mastonia—the church, the schoolhouse porch, the shelves in Sonny Ray's store. They were his testimony. Proof that a man who had been counted as property could make something permanent.

The arthritis had come on slow, the way all cruelties of age do. First a stiffness in the mornings. Then a catch in his grip that made him drop things—a hammer, a cup, his wife's hand. By the time the stranger arrived, Thornton's fingers had curled into themselves like dead leaves, the knuckles swollen and hot, the joints fused into a permanent almost-fist. He could not hold a tool. Could not button his own shirt. Could not do the one thing that had made him Thornton.

The stranger found him on his porch, staring at his hands.

"Those hands built something beautiful," the Whistling Man said. "It seems unfair that they can't anymore."

Thornton said nothing.

"I could give them back to you. The strength. The steadiness. Hands like you had at thirty." The stranger sat beside him uninvited. "All I'd need in return is one memory. Just one. The day you don't need anymore."

Thornton thought about it for three days. On the fourth morning, he couldn't get his shirt buttons through the holes, and he wept with frustration—the quiet, furious tears of a man who had survived too much to be undone by his own fingers.

He went to the stranger that night.

In the morning, his hands were new. The swelling was gone. The joints moved smooth and easy, the fingers straightening, curling, stretching with a fluidity that made him laugh out loud. He picked up a hammer from the tool shelf and felt the weight of it settle into his palm like a handshake from an old friend.

He walked to the church. Stood in front of it.

He knew he had built it. The knowledge was there—factual, certain, documented in Etta Mae's ledger. But the memory was gone. The morning the walls went up. The hymns the women sang while the men worked. The smell of fresh-cut pine and sweat and the red clay dust that had coated everything. The moment the last beam was set and the men had stepped back and looked at what their hands had made—the silence that had fallen, holy and full, the silence of men who had been property realizing they had built something that would outlast them all.

Gone. All of it.

He stood in front of a building his hands had raised and felt nothing. The church was a fact. It used to be a miracle.

* * *

The Widow Carson went to him on a Wednesday.

Everyone in Mastonia knew Nettie Carson by her voice—not its sound, but its purpose. Since Raymond's death eight years ago, she had become the keeper of his memory. At every gathering, every church supper, every quiet moment on a neighbor's porch, she was the one who said "Raymond used to say..." and brought him back into the room. She told the stories so often that children who had never met the man could describe the scar on his chin from a boyhood fall, the way he tilted his head when he was listening, the laugh that started in his belly and worked its way up until his whole body shook with it.

It was her purpose. Her ministry. The thing that got her out of bed on mornings when the empty side of it threatened to pull her back down.

But the telling was also the wound. Every story she told was a reminder that she was talking about a man who would never talk back. Every detail she preserved was a detail she had to carry alone. She had not slept through the night in eight years. Her hand still reached for him in the dark. Her body still waited for a weight on the mattress that would never come.

The stranger came to her house in the evening, when the loneliness was worst.

"You carry him so well," he said from her front gate, not coming closer. "But it's heavy, isn't it? Eight years of carrying a man who can't help you hold him."

"Don't you talk about Raymond."

"I'm not talking about Raymond. I'm talking about you." His voice was gentle. "I can give you rest, Mrs. Carson. Real rest. The kind where you close your eyes and don't reach for anyone. The kind where morning comes without the empty side of the bed being the first thing you feel."

She held out for two days.

On the third night—after waking at two in the morning with her hand on his pillow and his name on her lips—she went to the boarding house.

She slept through the night for the first time in eight years. Slept deep and dreamless and woke feeling something she had forgotten existed: rested. Whole. The ache in her chest had eased. The weight had lifted.

At the church supper that Sunday, she opened her mouth to tell a Raymond story—the one about the fishing trip, the one that always made people laugh—and stopped. She knew the words. She knew what happened, who said what, how the day had ended. But Raymond's face would not come. She reached for it the way you reach for a light switch in a familiar room, and found only wall. The scar on his chin. The tilt of his head. The laugh that started in his belly. All of it—flat. A description where a person used to be.

She was describing a silhouette. The words were there. The man behind them had gone.

Nettie Carson stopped telling Raymond stories after that. People noticed. They said grief had finally caught up with her, that she was learning to let go. They meant it kindly. They did not understand that she had not let go of Raymond. She had been emptied of him. And the difference between those two things was the difference between setting down a burden and having it stolen from your hands.

* * *

Then young Samuel Oakes, who had lost his arm in a farming accident and would have given anything to be whole again.

Each of them sought out the stranger in the night. Each of them crossed a threshold they could not uncross. Each of them came back changed—if they came back at all.

The mother vein pulsed at night now. People living near the ridge reported strange dreams. Voices in the crystal. Names being called from underground. Some swore they heard Marcus Webb, calling for help in a voice that could not quite remember how to speak.

Etta Mae wrote it all down. Every disappearance. Every change. Every name that started slipping from collective memory. Her ledger grew thick with entries. Her hands cramped from the work. But she did not stop.

She couldn't stop. If she stopped, the forgetting would win. If she stopped, it would be like they had never existed at all.

"He is collecting us," she told Sonny Ray late one night. The store was closed. The streets were empty. The whistle drifted down from somewhere up the ridge, patient and endless. "Not killing. Collecting. Taking what makes us us and... and filing it away somewhere. Like specimens in a jar."

"What does he want with us?"

"I do not know. Maybe nothing. Maybe everything." She closed the ledger gently. Ran her fingers over the leather cover that had gone soft from forty years of handling. "Maybe he is just the kind of thing that takes because taking is what it does. Like a fire burns. Like a river floods. Maybe there is no why.

Just is."

Sonny Ray reached across the counter. Took her hand. His fingers were rough and warm and real. "Whatever happens," he said quietly. "I am glad I got to know you, Etta Mae Crawford. I am glad I got to love you, even if I never did say it right."

Her eyes burned. "You say it fine, Sonny Ray Williams. You always have."

Outside, the whistle rose and fell. Patient. Waiting. Like it had all the time in the world.

Because it did.

* * *

8

The Pattern

Etta Mae saw it first.

Not the bargains themselves—those were happening behind closed doors. But she saw the aftermath. The small changes. The gaps where something should have been.

Marcus Webb had been the first sign. Before he vanished entirely, he could no longer remember his father's voice.

Martha Gable's roof was fixed—beautiful, solid work that seemed to have appeared overnight. But when Etta Mae asked about her wedding day, Martha's eyes went distant.

"I was married," she said. "I have the ring. The certificate. But the day itself..." She shook her head. "It's like trying to remember a dream."

Young Thomas Crawford had stopped talking about leaving. Had stopped dreaming about Chicago.

"I just... don't feel it anymore," he said. "The wanting. I know I used to want to go. I just can't remember why."

Etta Mae wrote it all down. Every bargain she could identify. Every loss she could document.

And as she wrote, a pattern began to emerge.

The stranger wasn't taking random memories. He was taking defining ones. The moments that made people who they were.

He was taking pieces of their souls.

And they were letting him.

*　*　*

That night, she spread her notes across the kitchen table and stared at them until her eyes burned. She thought about Delphine's warning. It walks like a man. But it is not a man. She thought about the way he'd looked at her ledger. And slowly, terribly, she began to understand.

Marcus Webb: the day his father recognized him. Miss Lillian: the song she'd sung to her dying mother. Thornton: the morning he raised the church walls. Widow Carson: her husband's face. Silas: the moment he'd first held his daughter. Each bargain had taken the same thing—not just any memory, but the one that mattered most. The one that made them who they were.

And her ledger—her careful, comprehensive, forty-year record of every soul in Mastonia—was the most complete definition of all.

She had been writing an inventory.

She just hadn't known for whom.

***

9

The Town Divided

The community meeting was held days after the stranger's arrival. Deacon Willis called it.

They gathered in the church itself—the pews packed, people standing along the walls. The air was thick with fear and anger.

"We all know why we're here," Deacon Willis said. "The stranger. The Whistling Man, some are calling him. We need to decide what to do."

The room erupted.

"We should run him out of town—"

"He hasn't done anything illegal—"

"He's taking things! Taking memories!"

"Only from people who agreed to it!"

"ENOUGH." Sonny Ray's voice cut through the chaos. He stood up, his massive frame commanding attention. "We're not going to solve anything by shouting at each other."

The room quieted.

"We need to think this through," he said.

"We've got three choices, way I see it. We fight him. We run. Or we bargain."

"Bargain?" Old Thomas Crawford stood up, his face red. "You mean give him what he wants? After what he did to Silas?"

"Silas got his forge working. Martha got her roof fixed. Thornton can hold a hammer again. They agreed to the trades."

"They didn't know what they were giving up!"

"That's on him, not on us deciding what to do now." Sonny Ray looked around the room. "I'm not saying bargaining is right. I'm saying it's an option. Some folks might choose it."

"And fighting?" someone called from the back. "How do you fight something like that?"

Silence.

Etta Mae stood up.

"I don't think we can fight him," she said. "Not the way we'd fight a man. He's not... he's something else. Something old."

"Then what do you suggest?"

"I don't know yet." She looked at the faces around her—faces she'd known all her life. "But I'm going to find out. I've been documenting this town for forty years. Maybe it's time to document him."

The meeting ended without resolution. The town remained divided—some wanting to flee, some wanting to fight, some already quietly seeking out the stranger to make their own bargains.

Deacon Willis left town the next morning—one of his usual trips to the next county, this time to see about lumber for the church roof. He said he'd be back in a day or two.

* * *

10

The Revelation

Etta Mae walked home alone, the ledger heavy in her bag. The stranger was waiting on her porch.

He was sitting on her grandmother's swing, one leg crossed over the other, his perfect shoes catching the lamplight from inside. He smiled when he saw her.

"Good evening, Etta Mae," he said. "I've been hoping we could talk."

She did not invite him inside.

She stood on the bottom step, the ledger clutched against her chest.

"What do you want?"

"The same thing you want." He didn't stand.

Didn't move toward her. "To understand."

"I don't think we want the same things."

"Don't you?" He tilted his head. "You spend your life writing things down. Making them permanent. Making them real." His eyes seemed to see through her. "I appreciate that kind of work. I value it."

"You value my ledger."

"I value what you've built." He stood then, a fluid motion. "Forty years of names. Forty years of stories. Every person in this town, defined.

Documented. Made complete." He took a step toward her. "Do you know how rare that is?"

Etta Mae backed up. Her shoulders hit the porch railing.

"You're using them," she said. "The bargains. You're taking pieces of people—"

"I only take what's offered."

"You're manipulating them!"

"I make them nothing." His voice was still warm, but there was something underneath it now. Something old and patient and vast. "They come to me with their problems. Their pain. And I offer them a trade. A fair trade."

"They don't understand what they're giving up."

"They understand enough." He was close now.

"They understand that they want something, and they're willing to pay. That's consent, Etta Mae. That's all I need."

She thought about Marcus Webb, who couldn't remember his father's voice.

"What are you building?" she asked. "What are you collecting them for?"

His smile widened, slow and certain.

"I'm building a collection. A complete collection." He reached out—she flinched, but he only touched the leather of her ledger bag. "Names. Stories. The defined essence of every soul in this town. And when the collection is complete—when every person has been documented, witnessed, made real enough to be held—then Mastonia will be mine. All of it. Forever."

The words hit her like a physical blow.

"My ledger," she whispered. "You're using my ledger."

"You've been preparing my inventory for forty years." His voice was almost kind. "Every name you wrote. Every story you recorded. You made them collectible, Etta Mae. You made them complete enough to be claimed."

She wanted to run. Wanted to scream.

But she couldn't move.

"Why are you telling me this?"

"Because you asked." He stepped back. "And because it doesn't matter. You can't stop what's already happening. The collection is almost complete."

He tilted his head, as if listening to something far away. Something that hadn't happened yet.

"There's a young man down in Mississippi," he murmured. Not to her. "Practices at the crossroads every night. Hungry one." He pulled out a pocket watch—gold, old, the kind of thing that had seen centuries. Studied it. "But that's for later."

He put the watch away and looked at her one last time.

"Thank you, Etta Mae. For your service. For your holy work." His smile widened. "I couldn't have done it without you."

He walked off the porch and into the darkness.

The whistle faded into the night.

Etta Mae stood frozen on the steps, understanding at last what she had done.

* * *

Part Three: The Collecting

***

11

The Confrontation

Etta Mae went to him on the seventh night.

Not because she had been summoned. Not because she had changed her mind. But because waiting was its own kind of dying, and she had never been the type to die slow.

The walk to the quarry took longer than it should have. The roads that had been familiar her whole life seemed to shift beneath her feet, curving away from themselves, leading her in circles that only straightened when she stopped thinking about where she was going and just walked. The stranger's influence had seeped into the land itself, rewriting the geography of home into something uncertain and treacherous.

The moon was full. It hung above the ridge like an eye, silver and unblinking, casting shadows that moved wrong. Trees that should have stood still seemed to sway in a wind she couldn't feel. The crystal veins in the rocks glinted as she passed, throwing back her reflection in fragments—a piece of her face here, a piece there, as if she were already being divided into collectible parts.

She found him at the edge of the quarry.

Standing where the mother vein surfaced in a jagged ridge of crystal that caught the moonlight and threw it back in broken pieces. He was not whistling. Not smiling. Just standing there like he was listening to something only he could hear.

The crystal hummed. She could feel it through the soles of her feet, a vibration that traveled up through her bones and settled in her teeth. All the voices that had ever been sung into these stones— prayers and promises, names and secrets, the accumulated weight of generations—all of it pulsing beneath the surface like a heartbeat.

"Miss Crawford." He did not turn around. "I wondered when you would come."

"What are you?"

Now he turned. His face was still beautiful. Still wrong. In the moonlight, it looked almost transparent—skin stretched over something that did not quite fill it, features arranged in an approximation of humanity that became less convincing the longer you looked. The proportions that had seemed perfect in daylight now revealed themselves as something else: a mask, worn by something that had never needed a face before and did not entirely understand what faces were for.

"That is a complicated question. The short answer is: I am old. Very old. Older than your country.

Older than your language. Older than the names you use to sort the world into categories you can understand."

"That is not an answer."

"No. But it is true." He gestured at the crystal ridge. In the moonlight, the quartz looked like frozen lightning—jagged and sharp and somehow alive, shot through with veins of color that should not have been visible in the darkness. "Do you know what quartz does, Miss Crawford? It vibrates. At specific frequencies. It holds energy. Records sound. Stores memory. The old folks knew this. They sang into the stones because the stones would remember. Would keep their voices safe."

"And you? Do the stones keep you safe?"

His laugh was soft. Without warmth. A sound that arrived without breath, without lungs, without any of the biological machinery that made laughter human.

"I am not kept, Miss Crawford. I am the one who keeps. I find places like this, places where memory gathers, where identity pools, and I... preserve them. Take them somewhere they cannot be lost. Cannot be forgotten. Cannot fade away like everything else in your brief, bright little world."

"Preserve them. You mean consume them."

"Is there a difference?" His eyes caught the moonlight. No color. Just depth—wells that went down and down into darkness that had never seen light. "Everything that lives, dies. Everything that is built, falls. Everything that is remembered is eventually forgotten. I offer an alternative. Eternity, of a kind. Existence without ending. Your people, your names, your stories—all of it kept safe. Perfect. Unchanging."

"Unchanging." Etta Mae's voice was steady. Her hands were not. They hung at her sides, trembling with the effort of not reaching for him, not striking him, not doing something violent and useless. "You mean dead. You mean frozen. A butterfly pinned to a board. A flower pressed in a book. Pretty to look at.

Nothing underneath."

The stranger's smile flickered. Just for a moment. Like a mask that had slipped, revealing something beneath that had no expression at all.

"You are clever, Miss Crawford. Clever enough to see through the comfortable words. But not clever enough to understand what you are refusing." He stepped closer. His shadow fell across her, cold as well water, and she felt the temperature drop around her like stepping into a cellar. "Your town is dying. Has been dying since the trains stopped. In another generation, maybe two, there will be nothing left but names on headstones and a road that leads nowhere. I am offering to save you from that. To make sure Mastonia lasts forever."

"In your collection."

"In my care."

"Under your control."

"Under my protection."

The mother vein pulsed beneath their feet. Etta Mae felt it like a second heartbeat, steady and ancient, full of voices that had been singing into these stones for longer than anyone could remember. Her grandmother's voice was in there somewhere. Her mother's. Her sister's—Beatrice, who she had never reconciled with, whose funeral she had not attended, whose forgiveness she would never receive.

All of them, singing in the dark.

She looked at him. At this thing wearing a man's face, speaking a man's words, making a man's promises. And she thought about the ledger at home, full of names she had written down. Thought about the work her grandmother had placed in her hands forty years ago. Thought about what it meant to be the one who remembered, when remembering was the only weapon you had.

"No," she said.

The stranger's face went very still.

"No?"

"No. We do not accept. We do not consent. Whatever you are, whatever you want, you cannot have it. Not from me. Not from any of us."

"That is not how this works, Miss Crawford." His voice had changed. Gone cold. Gone old. The warmth had drained out of it like blood from a wound, leaving something that scraped against her ears like stone against stone. "I do not need your consent. Consent is a courtesy. A kindness. A way of making the transition easier. But I have taken towns that fought. Taken cultures that resisted. Taken entire peoples who swore they would never break." He leaned in. His breath was ice. "Everyone breaks eventually. Everyone falls. Everyone becomes part of my collection, whether they sign the paper or not. The only question is whether they do it with dignity or drag it out into something ugly."

"Then I choose ugly."

He stared at her. For a long moment, nothing moved. Not the wind. Not the crystal. Not the stars above. The world held its breath, waiting to see what would happen when an unstoppable thing met something that refused to move.

Then he laughed.

Not the warm, practiced laugh he had used before. Something else. Something that scraped against the inside of her skull like broken glass, that vibrated at frequencies the human ear was never meant to process. She felt it in her teeth. In her bones. In the deep places where fear lived.

"Very well, Miss Crawford. Ugly it is. But remember, when the screaming starts, that I offered you a choice. Remember that you could have made this easy. Could have laid down your burden and rested."

"I will remember everything." Etta Mae's voice did not waver. Her body was shaking—she could feel it, the tremors running through her like electricity— but her voice was steady as stone. "That is what I do. That is what I am. And long after you have taken everything else, I will still remember. I will remember your face and your voice and every lie you ever told. And I will write it down somewhere you cannot reach. And someday, someone will find it. Someone will read it. And they will know what you are. What you really are."

The stranger's smile was gone.

"We will see."

He turned and walked away. Into the darkness. Into the crystal. Into whatever hole in the world he had crawled from. His form seemed to blur at the edges as he moved, becoming less solid with each step, until he was just a shape, then a shadow, then nothing at all.

The mother vein went silent. The humming stopped. The night settled back into ordinary darkness, stars and moon and the distant sound of insects that had been too afraid to sing while he was present.

Etta Mae stood alone at the edge of the quarry. Her heart pounding. Her hands shaking. Her mind already composing the entry she would write.

August 21, 1926. Confronted the stranger at the quarry. He is not human. He is not from here. He collects towns like other men collect coins. And he will take Mastonia, all of it, unless we find a way to stop him.

I do not know if we can stop him.

But I know we have to try.

She walked home through roads that no longer curved away from her. The stranger's attention had shifted, moved on, begun preparing for whatever came next. She had bought time. How much, she didn't know. But enough to write. Enough to warn. Enough to make sure that whatever happened, someone would remember.

The ledger was waiting for her when she got home. The lamp had burned low but not out. The ink had dried on Opal Miller's entry.

She sat down. Picked up her pen. And began to write.

***

12

The Refused Bargain

On the seventh day, the Whistling Man came for Sonny Ray.

It happened at the store, in the hour before dawn when Sonny Ray was alone. The door opened without a sound. The shadows seemed to deepen. And then the stranger was standing between the shelves. "You've been avoiding me," he said.

Sonny Ray didn't look up from the crate he was unpacking. "I've been busy."

"We're all busy. That's the wonderful thing about time—there's never enough of it." The stranger walked closer. "Except for some of us. Some of us have more time than we know what to do with."

"What do you want?"

"What everyone wants. To help." The stranger stopped at the edge of the lamplight. "I understand you had a brother. Samuel. He went north. He didn't come back."

Sonny Ray's hands stopped moving.

"That's not something I talk about."

"Of course not. It's painful. Unresolved. You never found out who killed him. You never got justice." The stranger's voice was soft. "That kind of wound… it festers. You carry it everywhere, don't you?"

"Stop."

"I could help with that. The memory of waiting for that telegram. The moment you learned he was dead. I could take that moment away."

"And what would I owe you?"

"Only that. Only the memory." Sonny Ray was quiet for a long moment.

Then he laughed.

It was not a pleasant laugh.

"No," he said.

The stranger's smile faltered.

"No?"

"You want me to give up the worst moment of my life. The moment that made me who I am." Sonny Ray stepped forward. "Samuel's death—it broke something in me. But it also taught me something. It taught me that the world takes things. That you can't always protect the people you love. That sometimes all you can do is stand where you are and refuse to move."

He was close now. Close enough to see the stranger's eyes, which held no color anyone could name.

"You want my pain? You can't have it. It's mine. I earned it." He took another step. "And I'm not giving you anything else either. Not one memory. Not one name. Not one god-damn thing."

The stranger was no longer smiling.

"You understand," he said, and his voice was different now—colder, older. "Refusing me changes nothing. The collection will be completed. It always is."

"Maybe. But it won't be completed with my help."

"There are others. Your friend Etta Mae, for instance. Her ledger is very comprehensive."

"You stay away from her."

"I don't have to go near her. She comes to me. Every time she writes a name." The stranger's smile returned—thin, sharp. "She's been preparing my inventory for forty years."

Sonny Ray wanted to hit him. But he knew it wouldn't work.

"Get out," he said. "Get out of my store." The stranger stepped back.

"We'll speak again," he said. "When the collection is nearly complete. When you're one of the last names left."

He paused at the door.

"I remember this conversation," he murmured. "You were very brave. You will be." He smiled at his own words.

Then he was gone.

And Sonny Ray stood alone, trying to make sense of a sentence that seemed to come from the wrong direction of time.

* * *

13

Delphine's Misreading

Delphine threw the bones again on the morning of the tenth day.

The pattern was different. Worse.

"There's a way," she said to Etta Mae. "The bones are showing me a way to stop him."

They were in Delphine's cottage, the curtains drawn.

"What way?"

"He collects things. Defines them. Owns them." Delphine traced the bones with trembling fingers. "But what if something could not be defined?

What if there was a name that couldn't be written?"

"The quartz," Etta Mae said slowly. "You're talking about speaking into the quartz."

"The mother vein. If we could put something there—something essential—but not define it fully. He couldn't collect what he couldn't understand."

"What would we put there?"

Delphine was quiet for a long moment.

"A name," she said finally. "His name. If we could define him—name him, document him, make him as real as the people in your ledger—maybe the mountain could hold him."

"But we don't know his name."

"Names have power. But descriptions have power too." Delphine's eyes were bright. "You've seen him. You've watched him work. You could write down what he is."

"And that would stop him?"

"The bones say it's a chance." Delphine gathered the bones. "The bones say..."

She stopped.

Her face went pale.

"What is it?"

"The bones say I'm almost right." Her voice was barely a whisper. "Almost. Not completely."

* * *

They went to the mother vein that night.

Etta Mae, Delphine, and Sonny Ray—who had refused to let them go alone.

The mother vein was a mile outside town, deep in a hollow where the ridges came together. The quartz there was a solid wall of crystal rising from the earth, milky white and faintly luminescent in the moonlight.

Etta Mae opened her ledger to a blank page. "Tell me what to write," she said.

Delphine closed her eyes. She began to speak —describing the stranger's appearance, his manner, the wrongness of his presence. Etta Mae wrote it all down.

He is a Black man the color of midnight. Not shadow, not absence, but depth. His suit never wrinkles. His eyes hold no color anyone can name.

He speaks of opportunity like generosity. He makes deals, and he always keeps his word.

He collects.

He owns.

He—

Etta Mae stopped.

The quartz was glowing.

Not the soft moonlight glow of before. Brighter, pulsing.

"Delphine," Sonny Ray said. "Something's happening."

Delphine's eyes snapped open.

And then the Whistling Man was there.

He stood at the edge of the hollow, silhouetted against the moonlit ridge.

"How generous," he said. "To bring the ledger to me."

* * *

"You can't have it." Etta Mae clutched the ledger to her chest.

"I don't take things, Etta Mae. But you've been so kind. Writing everything down."

He tilted his head, listening to something only he could hear.

"The bones told you there was a way," he said to Delphine. "They showed you a chance." His smile widened. "But the bones don't explain, do they? They show what might be, not what will be."

Delphine's face was ashen. "They said—"

"They said you were almost right." His voice was gentle. Pitying. "Almost. That's the cruelest word, isn't it?"

He reached out and touched the quartz.

The glow intensified. The hum became a roar.

"You weren't trapping me," he said. "You were completing me. Giving me a definition. Making me part of the collection." He looked at Etta Mae. "My name is in your ledger now. And when I complete the collection of Mastonia, I'll be complete too."

Etta Mae understood then, with a horror that went deeper than fear. His power was in being undefined—a shape without edges, a hunger without name. The people he collected became complete in his keeping, finished and owned. But he himself had always remained outside that completeness, the collector rather than the collected. Until now. Until she had written him into existence the same way she had written everyone else.

Delphine made a sound—a gasp, a sob.

"I tried," she whispered.

"You thought the bones would save you." The stranger's voice was soft. "But the bones only show. They don't protect."

He turned to her, and his eyes were endless.

"Thank you, Delphine Rousseau, for your almost-right reading."

He reached out.

She had time to scream.

And then she was gone.

Not dead. Not transported. Just... gone.

Sonny Ray roared something wordless and lunged forward.

The stranger caught him with one hand.

"Not yet," he said. "Your turn comes later. When the collection is almost complete." He released Sonny Ray, who stumbled back.

"Run," the stranger said. "It doesn't matter. Documentation is how I win."

He walked into the darkness.

Etta Mae stood frozen, staring at the space where Delphine had been.

* * *

14

Sonny Ray's Stand

The collections accelerated after that.

Each day, another bargain. Another gap where a memory should have been.

Sonny Ray watched it happen. He couldn't stop it—couldn't be everywhere at once, couldn't talk sense into people who had already decided their pain wasn't worth keeping.

But he could refuse.

Every time the stranger appeared—in the store, on the road, at the edge of his property—Sonny Ray said the same thing.

"No."

"You're stubborn," the stranger said on the fifteenth day. "I admire that."

"I said no."

"Your friend Etta Mae is working so hard. Writing everything down. Making my inventory more complete with each

88

passing hour." The stranger smiled. "She can't help it. It's who she is."

"Leave her out of this."

"She was never out of it. She's been in it since before you were born."

* * *

On the twentieth day, the stranger came for Sonny Ray a final time.

It was evening. The store was closed. Sonny Ray sat on the back steps, watching the ridge line go dark, thinking about Samuel.

The stranger appeared without sound.

"It's almost over," he said.

"I know."

"You're one of the last. You and Etta Mae and a handful of others." The stranger sat down beside him—casual, familiar. "The collection is nearly complete."

Sonny Ray said nothing.

"I'm going to offer you one more time," the stranger said. "Not because I need to. Because I want to. Because you've earned it."

"Earned what?"

"The chance to make it easy. I can take the part of you that fights. The part that stands. I can make the end painless."

Sonny Ray thought about that. Thought about what it would mean to stop fighting.

He thought about Etta Mae. About the ice storm. About forty years of standing together.

"No," he said.

The stranger sighed. "I thought you'd say that."

"Then why'd you ask?"

"Because hope is part of what makes you collectible."

The stranger stood.

"You're going to watch, Sonny Ray. You're going to watch me take everyone you've ever known. And then, when you're the last one standing, I'm going to take you too."

"I know."

"Does that frighten you?"

Sonny Ray looked at him—at the endless depth of his skin, the white teeth, the eyes that held no color.

"Yes," he said. "But I'm going to stand anyway."

The stranger smiled.

"Good," he said. "That's what makes you worth collecting."

* * *

15

The Last Night

On the final night, the crystal sang.

It started just past midnight. A low hum that rose from the mother vein and spread through the earth like ripples through water. Everyone felt it. Everyone heard it. Even those who had sold pieces of themselves, given away names and memories and hopes—even they looked up from their empty-eyed existence and knew that something was ending.

The hum grew louder. It built on itself, layer upon layer, until it wasn't a hum anymore but a chord —a harmony of frequencies that should not have been possible, that vibrated at the edge of hearing and then beyond it, becoming something felt rather than heard. The walls of houses trembled. Windows rattled in their frames. Dogs howled and then fell silent, as if even their voices had been subsumed into the larger sound.

Etta Mae was in her kitchen, writing by candlelight. She had not slept in three days. The ledger was almost full now.

Page after page of names and dates and stories, crammed together in increasingly desperate handwriting.

She was recording Henry Bessemer's history— every piece of it she could remember, every story she had ever heard him tell.

Her hand moved across the page with a desperation that had nothing to do with speed and everything to do with completeness. Henry Bessemer.

Born 1836 in a cabin outside Savannah, Georgia. Mother's name: Ruth. Father: unknown, because his father had been the property of a man whose records didn't include such details. Freed in 1865. Walked to Arkansas with nothing but the clothes on his back and a piece of paper that said he was his own person now.

The ink was running low. She'd been writing for three days, emptying bottle after bottle, her wrist cramping and releasing and cramping again. The candle threw shadows that danced across the page like they were trying to read what she wrote. Every few minutes she had to stop and flex her fingers, work the stiffness out of knuckles that were too old for this kind of sustained effort. But she couldn't stop. If she stopped, she might not start again. If she stopped, the names might slip away before she could anchor them to paper.

The first scream came.

Not a human scream. Something else. Something that came from the crystal itself, as if the mountains were giving birth to grief.

The candle flame bent sideways. Stretched toward the window, toward the ridge, toward the source of the sound. The ink on the page she was writing began to move, the letters crawling across the paper like insects trying to escape.

She grabbed the ledger and ran.

Outside, the world had changed.

The sky was wrong—not dark but absent, as if the stars had been removed rather than hidden. Where they should have been, there was only emptiness: a void that the eye refused to focus on, that the mind slid away from like water off oil. The moon was still there, but it looked different. Hollow. As if something had scooped out its light and left only the shape behind.

The air tasted like copper and cold stone. It pressed against Etta Mae's skin, heavy and wet, and when she breathed it in she felt it settle in her lungs like silt.

And rising from the quarry, visible even from the town center, a column of light that was not light. A beam of something that ate illumination rather than producing it. It stretched from the earth to the sky, a pillar of absence that cut the world in half.

People were in the streets. Running. Screaming. Some stood frozen, their mouths open, their eyes fixed on the column, their bodies rigid with a terror too large to process.

"Etta Mae!"

Sonny Ray found her at the crossroads. His face was wild. Blood ran from a cut on his forehead— he must have fallen, or been struck by something in his flight. His hands found her shoulders and gripped tight, like he was afraid she might dissolve if he let go.

"The church," he gasped. "Everyone's gathering at the church. It's the only place with—"

He stopped. Stared past her shoulder.

She turned.

The Whistling Man stood in the middle of the street.

But he was not the man who had walked into town a week ago. He was not a man at all anymore. The suit was gone. The smile was gone. The beautiful, terrible face that had made people look twice and then look away—gone.

What remained was shape without substance. Form without flesh. A darkness that stood upright and looked at her with eyes that had never been eyes. It

had the outline of a person—two legs, two arms, a head—but within that outline was nothing. Less than nothing. A hole in the world where a person should have been.

"Did you think doors could stop me, Miss Crawford?" His voice came from everywhere. From the ground. From the sky. From inside her own chest, vibrating in the spaces between her ribs. "Did you think prayers and crosses and the names of your little gods would make any difference?"

"Everyone!" Etta Mae screamed. Her voice cracked on the word, but it carried. "To the church! Now!"

They ran.

Old and young. Fast and slow. Some carried children. Some carried each other. The darkness pursued but did not hurry. It moved at the pace of inevitable things. Glaciers. Tides. Death.

They made it to the church. Barred the doors with pews dragged across the entrance. Lit every candle—dozens of them, hundreds, tiny flames that pushed back against the dark but could not defeat it. Reverend Clemmons started praying in a voice that cracked and rebuilt itself over and over, words tumbling out of him like water from a broken dam.

Through the windows, they could see it happening.

Houses folding in on themselves. Not falling— folding, like paper, like origami, like someone was taking the structures that generations had built and compressing them into shapes that took up no space at all. Trees sinking into the ground. The earth itself pulling downward, as if something beneath was swallowing the town piece by piece.

The general store went first. Then the schoolhouse. Then the row of houses on Oak Street where the Miller family lived, where Opal had been born just weeks ago.

"He is taking everything," someone sobbed. "Everything."

"Not everything." This was Henry Bessemer. He had found his way to the front of the church, pushing through the crowd with a strength that should not have been possible for a ninety-year-old man. His body was frail, but his voice carried like thunder.

Henry felt the weight of his ninety years as he pushed through the crowd, but it was a familiar weight —the weight of everything he had carried, everyone he had outlived, every morning he had woken up surprised to still be breathing. His knees protested. His hip—the one that had never healed right after the fall in '09—sent sharp complaints up through his spine. But he kept moving. He had learned a long time ago that the body's complaints were just noise, background

chatter that you could listen to or ignore as circumstances required.

The faces around him were lit by candlelight and wet with tears. Some he recognized—children of children of people he had known when he first came to Mastonia. Some were strangers, young folks born after his memory had started to blur at the edges. But they were all his people. That was the strange truth of living this long: eventually, everyone was your people, because you had seen enough of them born and buried that the bloodlines stopped mattering.

His mother had taught him the songs. His mother's mother had taught her. The songs went back further than that—back to ships and shores and a place where the sky was a different color and the stars hung in different patterns. He didn't remember all of them. Ninety years had worn grooves in his memory, and some things had slipped through the cracks. But he remembered enough. He remembered the ones that mattered.

The candle flames bent toward him as he reached the front of the church. Bent like they recognized something in him. Bent like they were listening.

"Not if we do not let him."

He looked at Etta Mae. At Sonny Ray. At the hundred-odd faces crowded into the pews, lit by candlelight, wet with tears, tight with terror.

"The crystal sings because it holds voices. All the voices we ever spoke into it. All the names we ever gave it. He wants that too. Wants to add it to his collection. But crystal does not just hold. Crystal transmits. Crystal vibrates. Crystal speaks."

"What are you saying, Henry?"

"I am saying we sing. Right now. Louder than we have ever sung. We put our names into the air and let the crystal carry them. Not to him. Past him. Through him. To wherever voices go when they refuse to die."

"Will that work?"

"I do not know." His smile was thin and fierce, the smile of a man who had been fighting hopeless battles his whole life and had never learned how to stop. "But it is the one thing he did not offer to take. The one thing we still have that he cannot buy. Our voices. Our breath. Our will to be heard." He raised his hands. "Sing with me. Sing your names. Sing your families. Sing everything you are and everyone you love. Sing so loud that even if he takes this place, takes us, takes everything—the song will already be gone. Already be free. Already be somewhere he can never reach."

They sang.

Not hymns. Not spirituals. Something older. Something that came from the place before words, when song was the first language and rhythm was the first truth.

Etta Mae felt it rise up in her—a sound that had no name, that she had never been taught but somehow knew. It came from her belly, from her chest, from the deep place where her grandmother's voice still lived. She opened her mouth and let it out, and around her, others did the same.

They sang their names and the names of their parents and the names of their parents' parents. They sang the work they had done and the children they had raised and the loves they had known. They sang Mastonia into the air, into the crystal, into the earth itself.

The voices layered on each other. Built on each other. Harmonized in ways that should not have been possible, that defied the mathematics of music. A hundred voices becoming one voice. Two hundred and thirty-seven names becoming one name. An entire town, compressing itself into a single frequency that the crystal caught and held and amplified.

And the church shook.

The candles flickered. Some went out. Others burned brighter, their flames turning colors—blue, green, white—that fire had no right to be.

And the darkness pressed against the windows.

It had reached the church now. Etta Mae could see it through the glass—that absence, that void, that hole where the world used to be. It pressed against the walls like water against a dam, testing, probing, looking for cracks.

And one by one, the candles guttered and died.

But the singing continued.

Even as the roof began to crumble. Even as the walls began to fold. Even as the Whistling Man's voice rose above everything else, claiming, demanding, taking—the singing continued.

Etta Mae pressed her ledger against her chest. The leather was warm from her body heat. The pages were full of names that would not be forgotten, not if she had anything to say about it. She added her voice to the chorus, felt it merge with the others, felt herself becoming part of something larger than any individual could be.

Sonny Ray's hand found hers and held it. His fingers were rough and warm and real, and she squeezed back with everything she had.

Sonny Ray had never been a singing man. His voice was rough, pitched wrong, the kind of voice that made children giggle when he tried to join the hymns on Sunday morning. He'd learned early to mouth the words, to let others carry the melody while he stood silent, feeling the music move through him without adding to it.

But now, in the crumbling church with the darkness pressing in, he sang. He sang because Etta Mae was singing, and he would follow her anywhere, even into a sound he couldn't make beautiful. He sang because Henry was singing, and the old man's voice was fading, and someone needed to carry the weight he was setting down. He sang because the children were crying, and the walls were folding, and there was nothing left to do but open his throat and let whatever was inside come out.

His voice cracked. It wavered. It found notes that didn't exist and held them anyway. And Etta Mae's hand in his said what words never could: Stay with me.

Whatever comes next, stay with me.

Henry Bessemer sang words that had no English translation, words his mother had taught him in a Georgia cabin a lifetime ago. Words that had survived the ocean, and the auction block, and the long walk to freedom. Words that carried the weight of everyone who had ever spoken them, everyone who had ever needed them, everyone who had refused to be silenced. Kum ba yah. Kum ba yah. The words meant "come by here"—a plea and a prayer and a summons all at once. But it was not the meaning that mattered. It was the sound. The vibration. The way the syllables rose from somewhere deeper than memory.

And somewhere, deep in the crystal, the mother vein received their voices.

Held them.

Transmitted them.

Into the earth. Into the stone. Into the deep places where even collectors could not reach.

In the space between moments, the collected heard it.

They existed in a place that had no walls and no sky, only the awareness of each other and the terrible knowledge of what they had lost. Marcus Webb was there, reaching endlessly for a memory of his father's voice that no longer existed. Miss Lillian was there, her mouth shaping a song she could no longer remember. Silas was there, his hands opening and closing around the ghost of a daughter he had held once, just once, before the stranger came.

They were complete now. Finished. Every defining moment stripped away and catalogued, every essential truth extracted and preserved. What remained was the shell—the shape of a person without the substance that made them real.

But the singing reached them. Faint and fractured, filtering through from a world they were no longer part of. A song in a language older than chains, older than ships, older than the long theft that had brought their ancestors to this shore.

The collected turned toward the sound. They could not join it. But they could listen. And in the listening, something stirred that the Whistling Man had not anticipated.

The darkness swallowed the church.

The singing stopped.

Mastonia fell silent.

* * *

Part Four: The Silence

***

16

The Aftermath

After.

Five of them walked away from where Mastonia had been.

Henry Bessemer. Ruth Ann. Ezekiel. Pearl. Young Thomas Crawford.

They did not speak as they walked. There was nothing to say that the silence was not already screaming. The trees thinned around them—pine giving way to oak giving way to scrub grass—and the ridge fell away behind them like a wave receding from shore. The road, what was left of it, curved toward the place where other towns might still exist. Where people might still wake in the morning and go about their lives without knowing that somewhere close, something terrible had finished feeding.

Henry walked slower than the others.

Each step sent pain through Henry's hip, up his spine, into the base of his skull where it settled like a coal refusing to cool. He had been walking for hours now. His legs wanted to stop, wanted to fold beneath him and let the road take him the way it had taken so many others. But the road wasn't done with him yet.

The story wasn't done being carried.

The others moved ahead of him—younger, faster, their grief expressed in the urgency of their movement. Henry understood that urgency. He had felt it himself, once, when flight seemed like the only sane response to catastrophe. But he was too old for flight now. Too old for anything but this steady, painful, deliberate putting of one foot in front of the other.

The cane helped. Ruth Ann had carved it for him years ago, from a branch of the oak tree that grew beside the church—the church that wasn't there anymore, that existed now only in the memories of those who had walked through its doors. The wood was smooth under his palm, polished by years of holding. It knew his hand the way his hand knew his grandmother's songs: through repetition, through necessity, through the simple fact of having been held so long that letting go was unthinkable.

His cane tapped against the packed earth in a rhythm that seemed to argue with the silence—tap, tap, tap—a heartbeat for a town that no longer had one. Every few steps, his lips moved. Words no one else could hear. Words that had survived the ocean, the auction block, the Georgia cabin, and now this.

He was praying. Or cursing. Or both. In languages like his, the line between the two was thin.

Ruth Ann glanced back once. Only once.

The ridge was still there. The sky above it was ordinary—just dawn light, pink and gold, the kind of sky that belonged in paintings. No column of darkness. No hum of crystal. Just morning, proceeding as if nothing had changed.

But the place where the town had been was gone. Not destroyed. Gone. As if Mastonia had been a word written on a chalkboard and someone had wiped it clean.

"Do not look back." Henry's voice was hoarse. Cracked at the edges like old leather. "Nothing good comes from looking back at a place that does not want to remember you."

They walked until the sun was high. Found a creek—narrow, cold, musical over stones that had been smoothed by centuries of water. They drank. The water tasted like minerals and cold stone, like the deep places of the earth where light had never reached.

Pearl cupped her hands and brought the water to her face, letting it run down her cheeks like tears. Her own tears had stopped hours ago. She had cried until there was nothing left, until her body had given up on grief and settled into a numbness that felt worse.

Ezekiel sat apart from the others, his back against a cypress trunk, staring at nothing. He was young—twenty-three, the youngest of the survivors— and his face had aged ten years in a single night. The lines around his eyes. The set of his jaw. The emptiness behind his gaze.

"We need to decide what to do," Young Thomas said finally. His voice was cracked now.

Smaller. The voice of a young man who had spent his whole life in this community and had just learned that belonging wasn't enough to save you. "We need to... to figure out..."

"There is nothing to figure." Pearl's voice was flat. Emptied out. "Everyone is gone. Everything is gone. What is there to decide?"

"She is right." Ezekiel's hands hung between his knees. He looked at them like he had never seen them before, like they belonged to someone else. "What is left? What do we even have anymore?"

"Each other." Henry had not sat down. Had not rested. He stood apart from the others, his eyes fixed on the road ahead, on the curve of earth that led away from everything they had known. "We have each other. We have our names. We have the story of what happened."

"What good is a story when nobody will believe it?"

"Stories do not need to be believed." Henry finally turned to look at them. His eyes were ancient. Terrible. Alive with something that might have been anger or might have been hope or might have been both. "Stories just need to be told. Belief is a luxury. Belief is what people can afford when they are safe and comfortable and certain that the things in the dark will never come for them." His jaw tightened. "We are not safe. We are not comfortable. And we are certainly not certain of anything anymore. So we tell the story without asking for belief. We tell it as a warning. We tell it as a wound that refuses to close."

"And then what?"

"Then we tell it again. To different people. In different places. We scatter it like seeds and hope that somewhere, someday, it grows into something that can fight back."

* * *

They found the marker three days later.

It was not where they had left it. It could not be where they had left it, because where they had left it no longer existed. But there it was, standing in a clearing half a mile from where the road bent toward Little Rock. Stone. Unadorned. Bearing only four words:

A TOWN WAS HERE

Pearl touched it first. Her hand trembled against the cold surface, and the stone seemed to vibrate beneath her palm—a frequency so low it was almost a feeling rather than a sound.

"I can feel them," she whispered. "All of them. Pushing against the inside of the stone. Trying to get out."

"They cannot get out." Henry's voice was gentle. Tired. The voice of a man who had been carrying weight for too long and had finally accepted that he would carry it until he died. "But they are not gone either. The crystal carried their voices. The stone holds their names. It is not living. It is not free. But it is not nothing."

"What is it, then?"

"A compromise." He limped forward and placed his own palm against the marker. Closed his eyes. His face changed—softened—as if he were hearing something the others could not. "The collector got his collection. But we... we got this. A piece that does not quite fit. A fragment that refuses to be filed away completely." His eyes opened. "It is not victory.

It is not even survival, not really. But it is something. Something he did not expect. Something he could not fully claim."

Young Thomas knelt beside the stone. His lips moved—not quite prayer, not quite anything he recognized. The words that came out were not words he had ever spoken before. They were older. Stranger. They sounded like the words Henry sometimes muttered under his breath, words that had no English equivalent.

"What are you saying?" Ezekiel asked.

"I do not know." His face was wet with tears he hadn't realized he was crying. "The words are just... coming. From somewhere. Like they were waiting for someone to speak them."

"The crystal." Henry nodded slowly. "The voices in the stone. They are still singing. Still trying to be heard. And sometimes, if you are empty enough, quiet enough, they can speak through you."

"That is..." Pearl shook her head. "That is impossible."

"Everything is impossible." Henry's smile was thin and tired and absolutely certain. "Until it isn't."

* * *

They could not stay together. That was clear within the first week.

The roads were being watched. Not by men— by something else. A feeling of attention. A sense of eyes that had no pupils. Whenever they camped as a group, the nights grew colder. The shadows grew longer. The whistle drifted down from ridges that should not have been close enough to hear.

"He knows we survived," Ruth Ann said on the seventh night. They were huddled around a fire that seemed too small to push back the darkness, eating roots and berries that tasted like nothing. "He is... hunting us. Trying to finish the collection."

"He cannot finish it." Henry was certain. "We are incomplete. Undefined. The stories we carry are fragments, not wholes. The memories we hold are damaged, confused, tangled with grief and shock. He collects complete things. Perfect things. We are neither."

"Then why is he hunting us?"

"Because we are loose threads." Henry stared into the fire. The flames reflected in his eyes, dancing, dying, being reborn. "Because loose threads can be pulled. Because the story we carry can grow, can spread, can become something larger than the collection that spawned it." His voice dropped. "Because collectors hate reminders that their collections are not complete. And we are a reminder. Walking. Breathing. Refusing to be filed away."

The fire crackled. An owl called somewhere in the darkness. The world continued on around them, indifferent to their grief, their fear, their desperate need to make sense of what had happened.

They decided to scatter. Five people going four different directions, each carrying a piece of the story. If one fell, the others would continue. If one was silenced, the others would keep speaking. It was not a plan. It was barely even a strategy.

Ruth Ann would go south. Ezekiel would go east. Pearl and Young Thomas would go west together —they had been circling each other since before the fall, orbiting like planets around a shared gravity, and now there seemed no point in pretending otherwise.

Henry would go north. Alone. With his cane and his fragmentary memories and the words his mother had taught him in a Georgia cabin before the war. His mind was slipping—had been slipping for months now—and he knew he would not find his way back to this place even if he tried. The fragments would scatter further. But the song would remain.

"We will not see each other again," Pearl said before they parted. It was not a question. The firelight caught the tears on her face, turned them gold, turned them into something almost beautiful.

"Probably not." Henry did not soften the truth. He had lived too long to believe in softening. "But we will be in the same story. And stories last longer than people."

They embraced. Awkwardly. Desperately. Five survivors who had been neighbors and now were something else.

Something that had no name yet because names were dangerous and definitions could be collected.

Ruth Ann held Pearl longest. Pressed her forehead to Pearl's forehead. Breathed the same breath for a moment, the way her mother had taught her to do with people you might never see again.

"Tell it true," she whispered. "Tell it whole.

Make them remember us, even if they never knew us." "I will," Pearl promised. "I swear I will."

And then they walked away.

Four directions.

Five threads.

One story, scattering like seeds on the wind.

* * *

The seeds did not take root.

One by one, in the weeks that followed, the five who had walked away stopped walking. Ruth Ann vanished from a boarding house in Shreveport, Louisiana, her bed still warm, her shoes still by the door. Ezekiel was last seen on a road outside Memphis, talking to a well-dressed stranger. Pearl and Young Thomas made it as far as Oklahoma before the whistle found them— found them together, holding hands, as if that could save them from what was coming.

Henry lasted longest. His mind, already fragmenting, made him difficult to pin down—difficult to define. He wandered for months, singing songs in languages he couldn't remember learning, leaving pieces of himself in every town he passed through. When he finally stopped, it was not because the Whistling Man caught him. It was because there was nothing left to catch. He had scattered himself so thoroughly that there was no collection to complete.

The only survivors were those who had never been there at all.

* * *

17

What Remains

The silence that settled over Mastonia was not merely quiet. It was the sound of a name trying to scream itself from inside a stone.

* * *

Four people stood at the edge of where the town had been.

Old Martha, who had been at her sister's place in Little Rock. Young Samuel, who had run away three weeks before. Deacon Willis, who had been in the next county. And a woman named Clara who had been visiting her daughter in Hot Springs.

Four people out of two hundred and thirty-seven.

They had come back to find nothing.

No foundations. No church. No schoolhouse. The quartz was gone too. The mother vein—just dirt now.

What remained was a single marker. Stone, unadorned. It bore no names. It said only:

A TOWN WAS HERE

Martha pressed her palm flat against the stone. It was cool. Solid. Real.

For a moment—one moment only—she thought she felt something.

The stone was cold under her palm—colder than it should have been in the August heat. She could feel something moving beneath the surface, a vibration that traveled up through her wrist and into her arm, settling in her shoulder like an ache that had always been there waiting to be named. The quartz in the marker held light differently than ordinary stone. It seemed to swallow the afternoon sun and hold it, refusing to give it back, keeping something bright and terrible locked away inside itself.

A vibration too faint to be certain. A hum that might have been her own pulse echoing back.

Or might have been two hundred and thirty-seven voices, pressed so tightly together they became a single frequency. Might have been Mastonia, still trying to say its own name from inside the stone.

She pulled her hand away.

The marker said nothing.

Markers never do.

* * *

They tried to speak the name.

Each of them, one by one.

The word was there—they knew it was there— but when they tried to push it past their teeth, something else came out. A cough. A grunt. Silence.

The name had been collected along with everything else.

"Mas—" Samuel tried, his young face contorting with effort.

Nothing. The second syllable caught in his throat like a fishhook.

They stood in the silence of a word that could no longer be spoken.

* * *

The roads that had led to Mastonia now wandered.

You could walk toward where it had been and never arrive.

They couldn't prove to anyone that a town had existed here. A real town with real people who had mattered.

All they had was the marker. And each other. And the knowledge that everything they had done to resist—every name documented, every story preserved, every voice spoken into the quartz—had been the very thing that completed his collection.

Their resistance was his receipt.

Their remembrance was his signature.

Their love was his final seal.

* * *

Epilogue

The road into Mississippi was dusty and long. Behind him, Arkansas was already fading—Mastonia just another name that no longer appeared on any map, another town that had been real once and now was not. There had been others before it. There would be others after.

The dust hung in the air like it was waiting for something. The road stretched in both directions— north toward Memphis and the factories that had

swallowed so many young Black men, south toward the Delta and its cotton and its particular forms of bondage. The crossroads itself was unremarkable: just a place where two dirt roads met, marked by nothing more than the old oak that had stood there longer than anyone could remember.

But there was a quality to the light here. A thickness to the shadows. The cicadas had gone quiet, and in their silence the evening seemed to hold its breath. Insects that should have been singing stayed mute in the tall grass. Even the wind had stilled, as if the air itself was listening for something that hadn't happened yet but was about to.

The quartz in his pocket hummed against his thigh. A frequency too low to hear but not too low to feel—a

vibration that seemed to come from somewhere deep in the earth, from the veins of crystal that ran beneath this land like frozen lightning, carrying voices, carrying names, carrying the compressed essence of everyone who had ever sung into their depths.

The Whistling Man walked it like heat didn't touch him.

In his pocket: a piece of quartz. Small. Unremarkable. But if you held it to your ear—if you were foolish enough to listen—you might hear something. Not silence. Containment. A whole town trying to scream its own name.

He stopped where the road split. An old oak twisted against the sky.

A young man sat beneath it, tuning a guitar. His fingers moved restless over the strings, searching for something they hadn't found yet. He looked up as the stranger approached.

"Evening," the Whistling Man said. His voice was warm. It always was.

"Evening." The young man's hands stilled on the strings.

"You play?"

"I try. Ain't nobody want to hear it yet."

The Whistling Man smiled. His teeth were very white.

"I know people. People who could make sure everybody hears it. Every juke joint from here to Chicago. Every radio in America. Your name in their mouths like a song they can't forget."

The young man's eyes flickered. Want. Hunger. The bone-deep need to be heard.

"What's it cost?"

The Whistling Man chuckled, warm as honey, soft as a hymn.

"Only what you're already willing to give."

The young man looked at his guitar. Looked at the crossroads. Looked at the stranger who seemed to belong to the settling dark.

He doesn't see the quartz in the man's pocket.

He doesn't hear Mastonia screaming.

The whistle came first.

It always does.

***

THE END

The whistling came first. But you stayed for what followed.